IDLENESS, SORROW, A FRIEND OR A FOE

A sequel to Who Knew the Storm

and

Who Knew the Storm: The New Generation

A book in two parts by Josephine Draycott

Woodbridge Publishers
1200 Century Way, Thorpe Park,
Leeds, LS158ZA

First Edition

ISBN (Paperback): 978-1-916849-87-7

ISBN (eBook): 978-1-916849-88-4

If applicable
Cover Design by Woodbridge Publishers.

Four be the things I am wiser to know:

Idleness, sorrow, a friend or a foe.

Four be the things I am better without:

Love, curiosity, freckles and doubt.

\- Dorothy Parker

PROLOGUE

Time does not bring relief; you all have lied

Who told me time would ease me of my pain!

I miss him in the weeping of the rain;

I want him at the shrinking of the tide;

The old snows melt from every mountain-side,

And last year's leaves are smoke in every lane;

But last year's bitter loving must remain

Heaped on my heart, and my old thoughts abide.

There are a hundred places where I fear

To go,—so with his memory they brim.

And entering with relief some quiet place

Where never fell his foot or shone his face

I say, "There is no memory of him here!"

And so stand stricken, so remembering him.

- Edna St. Vincent Millay

PART I

At Eternity's Gate

At Eternity's Gate, a painting by Vincent Van Gogh, dated May 1890

CHAPTER ONE

Torsten's torment

Torsten gazed listlessly out of the large, round window of the living room at the rain which was obscuring the normally stunning sea view. He was at a low ebb, just like the invisible tide below. He had been living alone in Bestefar's old cottage since the series of unfortunate events which had led to the permanent closure of the portal between the worlds, separating the Traansylvanians from their Earth friends forever, but it wasn't solitude that was killing him; it was grief.

He was missing Kim like a hole in his heart. The sea was a suitable companion for his restless soul: soothing at times, tempestuous at others, and he often spent hours just sitting on a bench near Baldursson's clifftop temple, staring at the waves and wondering if any of it had any meaning.

Not a day for sitting on a windswept bench today, however. The rain pattered despondently against the window pane as tears trickled down Torsten's blue-hued face, obscuring his vision even further. He thought wryly of Victor Hugo's words: "Those who do not weep, do not see."

"Ha," snorted Torsten, addressing the empty room and the rainstorm.

"Those who do weep don't see much either."

Smiling wanly at his little literary joke, he wiped away his tears and went to sit by the fire in the living room. It warmed his bones, and he sat back in his chair and closed his eyes, weary from weeping. Victor Hugo had put him in mind of Archibald Craven's well-stocked library back at Misselthwaite Manor. How he had loved that library. And Kim. He groaned and tried to turn his thoughts to other things.

Bestefar had a library too, but it was mainly filled with dusty, historical tomes of little interest to Torsten. Nonetheless, he decided to have another look and see if he could find something to read to while away the hours before bedtime.

He got up resolutely and walked down the hall to the library. It felt chilly after the warmth of the living room and smelt a mite musty. It was also dark, with shadows and memories lurking in every corner. Torsten shivered involuntarily and turned on some lamps. He remembered Bestefar's secret brannenmjød stash and poured himself a good measure of the swirling, amber liquid. He took a sip and felt the familiar, tingling warmth spreading through his body. He ran his hands idly over some shelves, then sat and turned over some dusty volumes lying on the equally dusty desk, which promptly made him sneeze.

An ornate cupboard in one corner of the room caught his eye (one of the four at least), so he drained his glass and crossed over to it, opening it gingerly as if afraid of what might be lurking behind the door.

It was a reassuringly cupboard-like cupboard, full of boxes and piles of books and what looked like photograph albums. He dragged these last items out, dusted them down and carried them back into the living room. He spent a couple of happy hours looking through them, wandering down memory lane. As a historian, Bestefar had been extremely good at record-keeping, and each album was meticulously labelled in chronological order. There were faded photographs of Bestefar, Bestemor, Torsten's parents, Gunnar and Agnes, then himself and Dordi at various ages, and finally Arne and Elea. Torsten lingered in particular over the faded photographs of his parents, captured during happy holidays at the cottage until the tragic sailing accident which had killed them when he was ten years old and Dordi just eight, leaving their grandparents to bring them up as best they could.

Drowsy from the heat of the fire, Torsten finally slept, waking with a start at first light, causing the photograph album still perched on his lap to fall to the floor. He groaned, yawned widely and bent down to pick it up. Stretching and muttering, he wandered over to the window and was pleased to see that the rain had finally stopped, and it promised to be a fine day.

After breakfast, he took a walk down to the beach and was invigorated by the salty breeze and the feel of the sun once more on his skin. Back at the cottage, he carefully carried the pile of photograph albums back to the library, which seemed more congenial in the light of day. He opened the cupboard and took out a box in order to push the bulky tomes back where he had found them. He rooted idly through the contents of the box. It contained a motley collection of dog-eared magazines, various coins and other random objects.

His curiosity was suddenly piqued by a smallish, metallic, black box which looked something akin to a remote control. A perfectly innocuous and not uncommon device under normal circumstances, but Bestefar did not have a goggle box in the cottage and had never shown the slightest inclination to have one. Torsten looked at it more closely. He thought he was imagining things at first but no, there it was again. It was blinking intermittently and emitting a very faint humming sound.

"Baldursson's beard," he said to nobody in particular.

He picked up the little black box and took it out of the library into the living room to get a better look at it. The humming sound was louder now, and the blinking more insistent. He moved into the kitchen, but nothing changed. As he walked towards the front door of the cottage, however, the box began vibrating slightly in Torsten's hand and the humming became more high-pitched.

Excited now, he went outside and stood in the garden. He rotated slowly on the spot, holding the device at arm's length to gauge its reaction.

As he turned towards the clifftop, it began vibrating vigorously, and the humming sound attained the dizzy heights of inaudibility. The mysterious object maintained these levels of agitated intensity as Torsten approached Baldursson's temple and finally peaked in a crescendo of fierce crackling as he reached Bestefar's grave, the headstone of which appeared to be emitting an eery, metallic glow.

Then, like the stuff of nightmares, the ground beneath the headstone began to heave and a great, gaping gash tore the earth asunder, rapidly increasing in size and heading directly towards where Torsten stood, rooted to the spot. As it reached his feet, he finally had the presence of mind to jump aside, but it was too late. He found himself falling into a deep, dark hole, losing his grip on the little black box as he went. He braced himself, assuming that he would land on Bestefar's coffin, but instead, he just kept on falling. And falling. And falling.

CHAPTER TWO

A rabbit hole to redemption

With a great whoosh and a flash of blue light, Torsten eventually landed on something soft. He felt like he'd literally been dragged through a hedge backwards. He realised that the "something soft" on which he had landed was protesting vociferously at this state of affairs, so he quickly rolled off it, groaned and opened his eyes painfully. He found he was lying on a beach. He licked his dry lips and could taste salt.

As his eyes adjusted to the bright light around him, he realised he was surrounded by green faces. Their bodies gradually swam sickeningly into his blurred vision. They were also green and very, very naked. He quickly realised that aside from their surprisingly large genitalia, they were also carrying very big spears.

The "something soft" on which he had landed, which turned out to be a terrified-looking Traansylvanian in a smart suit, whimpered and curled into a ball with his arms above his head as the very big spears came even closer. Torsten opened his mouth to scream, but suddenly the spears stopped in mid-air. The naked men were no longer green, but pink, and they were pointing at Torsten, waving their spears and whooping. Then they started chanting. Still shell-shocked, it took Torsten a while to understand that they were saying a name over and over again: Bestefar. He gaped. The chanting continued and he gaped some more. He realised that the man upon whom he had landed had uncurled himself from his protective ball and was gaping right along with him.

Suddenly, the chanting stopped and the group of men with spears parted to reveal a figure coming slowly across the beach towards them. As the figure came closer, Torsten saw that it was a woman, slightly bent and walking somewhat painstakingly with the aid of a stick. She was not naked, but clothed in a simple robe made out of some kind of woven material, and on her head she was wearing a woollen hat of indeterminate colour that looked like it had seen better days.

Her face was wrinkled and weather-beaten, but she smiled beatifically at Torsten and said, "Bestefar, ya has come back to us!"

Torsten opened his mouth to protest, but the insistent chanting had begun again.

It got louder and louder until the old woman finally waved her stick and yelled, "Will y'all jus' pipe down, now! You's givin' me a headache. And go an' put some clothes on. Y'all look ridiculous wid ya dongles danglin' in da wind dere."

The men with the impressive accoutrements looked sheepish then and wandered off towards a path between a clump of trees at the boundary of the beach, muttering to each other, their spears tucked under their arms.

The old woman addressed Torsten again with a toothless smile.

"Bestefar," she said, "it bin a long, long time."

Her speech had a strange, lilting quality unfamiliar to Torsten. She looked at the man still cowering on the sand beside him.

"And who be dis, den?" she asked.

Torsten was about to say he didn't have the foggiest idea who he was when the woman said, "He is strangely garbed to be sure. Is 'e your servin' man?"

Torsten looked at the man, who was gazing imploringly at him. He remembered that the men with spears had been busily pointing them at this man before he dropped in unexpectedly on the party. The woman seemed pleased enough to see him, but if she discovered that this dapper but dishevelled gentleman was not part of his tiny entourage, she may just call them back and let them do what they were planning to do with him in the first place.

"Erm, yes," he said, "but -"

The woman suddenly hugged him. He didn't hug her back and she looked at him reproachfully with her small, bright eyes.

"Bestefar," she said again, "Ya have forgotten me. I'm Lidia."

Torsten looked blank.

"Lidia," she repeated, and Torsten nodded dumbly.

"Forgive me, Bestefar, ya must be in need of refreshment after your journey," she said and turned in the direction the men with spears had taken, gesturing for them to follow.

Torsten helped the stranger up from the sand and they both stumbled after the bent figure hobbling ahead of them.

CHAPTER THREE

The Bestefarians

After a short walk, they emerged from the cover of the trees into a large, open space with wooden huts dotted around and, in the background, beautiful rolling hills that seemed to stretch far into the distance. The old woman stopped in front of one of the huts and, smiling, gestured with her stick for them to enter.

"A bath 'as been prepared for ya, Bestefar," she said. "Normally, ah would send some of ma men to attend ya, but since ya have your man here, I assume ya can manage. Rest now and we will summon ya for a celebratory feast at sundown."

And with that, she left.

Torsten entered the hut first and glanced around. It was surprisingly spacious and comfortable, with sleeping pallets on the ground and a large, metal bathtub steaming in the centre of the room. Torsten looked at it longingly, but the man in the suit had followed him in and collapsed down onto one of the sleeping pallets with his head in his hands. Torsten could see his shoulders heaving.

He saw a jug on a wooden table nearby and filled a cup with water. He handed it to the man, who took it with shaking hands. He took a couple of sips and then looked up tearfully at Torsten.

"Thank you," he said, sniffling. "You saved my life back there. Did Petra send you here too? She didn't send you to finish me off, did she, like in the Torminator?"

"The Torminator?" spluttered Torsten. "As in the film? Wait a minute, did you say Petra? Who the dritt are you?"

"Haakon," said the man morosely. "My name is Haakon."

Torsten did a comic double-take.

"Haakon," he said. "*The* Haakon?"

His face had gone a terrible shade of puce and he advanced upon the man before him, who appeared to have taken up cowering as a hobby, and who, in turn, had turned a rather ghastly shade of yellow.

"You," Torsten snarled, "are the reason why I can't see my friends on Earth any more. You're a greedy, little drittbag! Petra is my great-niece. I heard she'd banished you to the Otherland and good riddance! Wait a minute … this is the Otherland? Odin's blood! I've come back in time to the moment you were sent here. No wonder I feel like I've been through a heavy-duty wash cycle."

"But, but … I don't understand!" stammered Haakon. "How did you get here? I thought the portal was gone."

"So did I," replied Torsten, pouring himself a cup of water and taking a good slug, wishing it were something stronger.

He thought back to the remote control he had found and wished he hadn't.

"Looks like Bestefar may have been keeping some skeletons in his closet," he said thoughtfully.

"Bestefar," repeated Haakon, regaining some of his former composure, "That's what they were calling you. Why were they calling you that? What's your real name?"

"Torsten, if it's any of your business," Torsten replied testily.

"Uncle Torsten, of course," said Haakon. "Elea talked about you a lot."

They fell silent and Torsten paced the sandy floor of the hut while Haakon watched him nervously.

Finally, Torsten said, "I'm tempted to let those savages eat you after what you did, but they think you're my servant, so I'm not going to disabuse them of that notion for the moment. We'll find out more later when we're called for the feast, so in the meantime, I'm going to have a soak in that bath, and I suggest we both get some rest."

Torsten was shaken gently awake from a fitful sleep a couple of hours later by a man dressed in a loin cloth and a large, woollen hat similar to the one the old woman was wearing. He saw in the half-light that Haakon was sitting upright on his pallet, rubbing his eyes and stretching.

"Bestefar," said the man deferentially, in the same lilting tones as the old woman, "dinner is served if ya'd care to follow me."

"So you do wear some clothes after all," said Torsten, surprised and mildly amused by the man's get-up and civilised manners.

"Ya, man!" replied the messenger cheerfully. "Ya knows all dat naked stuff is jus' to scare off unwanted tourists. It's what *ya* told us to do, right?"

Torsten didn't know what to say at this juncture, so he said nothing.

The man looked at Haakon and said, "Your servant can stay here and he will be brought some food and wine."

Haakon looked like he was about to object, but Torsten gave him a meaningful look and said softly, "Stay here, and don't get up to any mischief."

He followed the man in the hat through the huts to an area filled with wooden tables and lit with flickering lamps. There was a smell of roasting meat in the air and another sweet, pungent aroma that he couldn't place. He saw the old woman standing nearby talking to a group of people, the men all in loincloths (long enough to preserve their modesty) and the women in robes similar to hers. All were wearing the same kind of wacky, woollen hat. She excused herself and hobbled over to Torsten.

"Bestefar," she gushed, "Ah hopes y'are well rested."

A man came over with a tray and she took two cups from it and handed one to Torsten.

"Ah's ordered our best wine served for da feast," she said.

He took a sip. It was the best wine he'd ever tasted.

"You are the leader, I gather," he said.

"Well, in a manner o' speakin'," she replied, looking at him quizzically. "Only in your absence, o' course. But now dat ya back …"

"Sorry," said Torsten, confused, "I thought that's what you said earlier on the beach, but my ears were still ringing from the effects of the crossing. Did you not say that you were the leader?"

She laughed, a pleasant tinkling sound that reminded Torsten suddenly of Dordi, his sister.

"Lidia," she said, "Ah was remindin' ya dat my name is Lidia. Does ya really not know me? Has it bin dat long, Bestefar?"

"Why do you keep calling me that?" he asked, genuinely perplexed. "My Bestefar is dead and gone, and you can't possibly have known him."

Lidia slapped her forehead.

"By da wool o' da ullabeist," she said, "but it really has bin dat long. Bestefar really mus' be dead an' gone. He was already old da last time 'e come 'ere. Ya can't be him!"

She looked unbearably sad for a moment. She put her wrinkled hand on Torsten's equally wrinkled cheek.

"But ya looks so much like 'im," she said.

Torsten looked more closely at Lidia. It was difficult to see in the light from the torches, but she certainly did bear a vague resemblance to Dordi. Was it possible, he wondered, that Bestefar had visited the Otherland? If so, why had he never said anything? He thought back to Kim's clandestine visit to Monet and came to the conclusion that anything was possible.

A woman with Lidia's bright eyes came up shyly and Lidia introduced her as her daughter Sophia. They moved together to a table at which an astonishingly beautiful young lady was already seated. She got up and curtsied to Torsten, who bowed courteously.

Lidia said, "Dis is ma granddaughter, Penelope. Penelope, dis is ….", she hesitated.

"Torsten," said Torsten, smiling.

"Not Bestefar?" said the girl, looking confused.

"Not Bestefar," said Lidia, sitting down carefully. "Let's eat, and we can work it all out afterward over a bit o' kaya."

Platefuls of food were brought to the table. Torsten realised that he was absolutely ravenous and gratefully fell on the delicious dishes that were put before him. Several cups of the excellent wine later, he was feeling better and beginning to like this place.

He turned to Lidia and said, "So what do you people call yourselves?"

"We are Bestefarians," she said, smiling her toothless smile.

CHAPTER FOUR

A pipeful of kaya helps the medicine go down

Once dinner was over, the younger children were shepherded off to bed and a group of musicians settled down nearby to play flutes mingled with small drums and wooden, stringed instruments Torsten had never seen before. He noticed that everyone was rummaging in small pouches they had tied around their waists and were pulling out what looked like clay pipes.

They began filling these pipes with some kind of tobacco, Torsten supposed, which had been placed on the tables in large pots. This reminded him sharply and painfully of Kim, who had loved his pipe. This was nothing like the mellow tobacco he used to smoke though. This had a strange, sickly sweet aroma and Torsten realised that this was what he had smelled earlier and had assumed to be something cooking.

A manservant placed a filled pipe before Torsten. He didn't touch it and Lidia looked at him expectantly.

He shook his head and said, "Actually, I don't smoke."

Lidia laughed her tinkling laugh, which made her sound so much younger, and said, "Ya man, everyone smoke here. It a social ting, y'kna, and it considered very impolite to refuse."

Torsten picked up the pipe gingerly and the same manservant quickly stepped up and handed him a taper lit from one of the nearby torches to light it. Torsten puffed experimentally on the pipe and exploded into a fit of coughing which made his companions explode into fits of uncontrollable laughter.

"T'is good, strong stuff an' no mistake!" chuckled Lidia, taking a good, long pull on her own pipe.

Torsten took a gulp of wine and tried again. This time felt better, smoother, and after a few more puffs, he was beginning to feel quite mellow about the whole thing. The music seemed sweeter somehow; it had a gentle but insistent rhythm that made him feel like bobbing his head along and he was comforted to see that many people around him were doing just that. Some were even getting up to dance, cavorting and gyrating to the hypnotic beat. He saw that Sophia and Penelope were among them, performing some kind of complex dance involving a great deal of arm waving that he himself would have been proud of.

He realised that Lidia was talking to him. She was sitting opposite him at the table, and seemed very far away, but very close at the same time.

"So Torsten," she said, rolling the name around her tongue as if tasting it to see if she liked it, "Ah has bin doin' some tinkin' and metink dat your Bestefar is da same as my Bestefar ... well ... (she gestured vaguely around her) ... *our* Bestefar."

"What do you mean?" asked Torsten.

His own tongue felt heavy and he was having difficulty articulating. He was still having this irresistible urge to bob his head along to the music, and he also had a sudden, unexpected craving for ice cream.

"Let's start at da very beginnin'" said Lidia in a sing-song voice.

"That's a very good place to start," responded Torsten, not quite knowing why, but it seemed like an entirely logical thing to say.

Could be a nice way to begin a song, he thought, and tucked the idea away for later.

Lidia nodded approvingly and began at the beginning:

"Da First Comin' o' Bestefar was long, long before ah was born. He arrive on our islan' in a beautiful sailin' boat. People tink dat 'e was da first to civilise us, but actually, my Bestemor had already started da process when she crossed da Odd Sea wid her parents an' dey landed 'ere. By da time Bestefar arrived, we was already learnin' da lingo, an' Bestemor was teachin' us to make clothes. Bestefar taught us his lingo too, and we eventually made a kind o' mishmash between da two, which is our lingo, an' we likes it.

Bestefar fell in love wid my Bestemor, Anthe, but 'e had another love 'e was already promised to back where 'e come from, and 'e felt bad about adandonin' her an' went away, nearly breakin' my Bestemor's heart and leavin' behind only 'is sailin' hat, or so 'e tought. A few month later, she gave birth to a beautiful baby girl, who was my moder, Eleftheria. I was jus' a slip of a ting not much older dan Sophia is now at da Secon' Comin'. He arrived not in a boat this time, but in a big flash o' blue light, just like you and ya manservant did today, by all account. Bestefar's oder love had passed away ya see, and 'e said 'e always felt bad about leavin' my Bestemor, so he came back hopin' to see her. My moder was angry wid him at firs' but 'e seemed so sad because my Bestemor had also passed not long since, and was so over da moons to find out dat 'e was not only a daddy, but also a grandaddy, dat she forgive 'im. He taught us da words Bestefar and Bestemor. He spent a bit o' happy time wid us but den 'e said 'e had to go home as 'e was needed back dere. Everyone loved him as much as dey had da first time and my moder set up a cult in his honour and we became Bestafarians. We all wear da sacred hat, which we make from da wool of da ullabeist, which live in da hills hereabout. And I always tought dat 'e might come back one day, so when you arrived, ah kin' of assumed … stupid really."

She laughed her tinkling laugh again.

Torsten was by now feeling too mellow to be shocked by any of this, even the fact that Bestefar had had a child with a woman other than Bestemor. He had listened intently to Lidia, munching all the while on a series of sweet things, brought this time by a pretty serving girl. He was, however, curious.

"So why did none of you ever travel over the sea to find him? It's not so far. Do you not have boats?" he asked.

"Nah, man," she said, sucking in her already hollow cheeks. "We 'as everytin' we need right 'ere. My Bestemor said she and her parents 'ad an awful, rough ride over da Odd Sea to get 'ere and after what Bestefar told us about da land where 'e lived, it all sounded so complicated, we never wanted to go dere. An' also," she added, laying down her spent pipe, "He never said as much, but we assumed 'e had family and dat's why 'e went back. We didn't want to make tings awkward. But ah really tink dat you are his grandson, ya look so much like him. As ah is his granddaughter."

"So we are cousins," said Torsten.

He did his old jazz hands thing, he was so thrilled.

"Seem dat way," smiled Lidia.

She stood up slightly unsteadily, leaned heavily on her stick and said, "An' now, time for bed. We can talk more tomorrow."

Torsten got up equally unsteadily.

"Woah," he said, grabbing at the table for support. "What is that stuff anyway?"

He pointed shakily in the direction of the pot on the table containing the pungent tobacco.

"Oh, dat kaya," she said matter-of-factly. "It a plant we grow 'ere. We use it to make our clothes, but it also pack a punch in a pipe, don' ya tink?"

Torsten nodded. He suddenly felt terribly weary.

"G'night, Lidia," he said.

"Sweet dreams, cuz," she said and wobbled off into the night.

Torsten eventually found his way back to his hut and flopped down onto his pallet. He was desperately sleepy but could hear laughter and smell kaya smoke drifting through an opening at the back of the hut near where Haakon should be sleeping.

He went out to investigate and found Haakon getting it on in the moonlight with a girl. They were sitting side by side on a bench, sharing a clay pipe, and Haakon had his arm around her. He was whispering in her ear and she was giggling. He sensed Torsten's presence behind him and turned abruptly, causing the girl to do the same and then jump up in a guilty panic. Torsten recognised her as the rather sweet serving girl who had served the sweet things after the meal. Before he had a chance to speak, she had run off like a frightened sneglhund, taking the pipe with her.

"Way to ruin a party," said Haakon, heaving himself up and squinting blearily at Torsten.

"Sorry," said Torsten, "But I thought I told you to keep out of mischief."

"Aaaah, but she's not a chief," said Haakon, attempting to tap the side of his nose but missing.

"She's a serving girl and she's sweet as sugar and her name is Calypso."

"Okay, Romeo," said Torsten, though this reference was entirely lost on Haakon, "Time for bed. We'll talk about this in the morning."

As Torsten was on the verge of slumber, Haakon whispered, "Torsten, do you still have the console?"

"The what?" he mumbled sleepily.

"The little black box," replied Haakon, "'cause I still have the bracelet."

"No," said Torsten. "I lost it during the crossing. But you can't go back, you know. You've really burned your bridges in Traansylvania."

Haakon thought about this.

"Oh well," he said eventually, "I think I might just stick around here for a while anyway."

But Torsten was already fast asleep.

CHAPTER FIVE

Island Time

The days passed in a pleasant haze and Torsten and Haakon began to fall easily into the island rhythm of life. Despite Torsten's dislike of Haakon, he had decided that it was easier to keep up the pretence that he was his manservant rather than denounce him. He knew that the Bestefarians would not want him on the island if they knew what he had done and Torsten was afraid of what they might do. Besides, he was enjoying himself and had no desire, at present, to rock the proverbial boat.

Haakon was enjoying himself too. As Torsten's 'manservant', he was only expected to tend to Torsten's needs, and he didn't have any, so he played his part, did his bit and kept the hut tidy, generally keeping out of Torsten's way. Calypso appeared to have him under some kind of spell. He was crazy about her and followed her around like a lovesick sneglhund. The servants were well-treated on this island, but they had plenty of work to do, so Calypso would gently shoo him away, and while she was working, he would lie on the beach or swim in the warm, turquoise sea. And think about Calypso.

Torsten spent a lot of time with Lidia and Sophia. Penelope was young and hung out with her own group of friends when she wasn't working. Lidia wasn't able to walk well with her stick, so he went on long walks around the island with Sophia, who was a little shy at first, but very good company once you got to know her. They walked up into the hills and saw the ullabeistene from which the Bestafarians took the wool to make their sacred hats and other clothes for the colder weather.

"It gets cold here?" asked Torsten, surprised.

"Not really cold," replied Sophia. "It's warm at this season, but later on, the days and especially nights can get cooler."

They walked right over to the other side of the island and Torsten was surprised to see that the sea was pink here.

"Dat is da Odd Sea," declaimed Sophia solemnly.

"It's pink," said Torsten, fairly uselessly. "Is that why it's odd?"

"Da pink colour is caused by da plants dat grow under da water. But dat not why it odd. It full o' dangerous currents and worse still, full o' strange creatures, da like o' which ya never seen before. Or want to see, for dat matter."

Torsten wanted to know more, but Sophia seemed genuinely ill at ease, so they began the long walk back to their village.

Breakfast was eaten late by Traansylvanian standards and Torsten never saw Lidia in the morning, as she liked to sleep in and then take a bath. He was often out walking for the rest of the day and carried a simple lunch with him, but he was always happy to see Lidia at dinner and, after having time to digest what he had learned on the first night, he had many questions to ask her about Bestefarian life over a pleasant pipeful of kaya.

He understood the reasons why they had not gone chasing after Bestefar to the mainland. But he did wonder why they didn't get any visitors from overseas. Lidia told him that the voyage over the Odd Sea was perilous and the only people she knew who had survived it were her Bestemor and her parents. As for the

Traansylvanians, she only knew what Bestefar had told her: that they weren't interested in the Otherland, but that if any unexpected visitors were to show up, they should act like dumb savages and scare them off, if possible. Hence the welcome Haakon, and subsequently Torsten, had received upon their arrival.

Torsten had also noticed another strange thing.

"Where are your husbands. Or partners?" he asked. "I'm presuming that Bestafarian reproduction occurs in the same way as in my country."

He blushed a little purply-pink at this. Lidia giggled like a girl.

"We don' have husbands," she tinkled merrily, "though we do fall in love an' sometime keep a partner for a while. But we are free to be wid whom we choose. Dere is no jealousy 'ere, an' most of our children are born as a result of da fertility rites."

Torsten raised his eyebrows.

He hesitated before asking his next question: "And are you allowed to love someone of the same sex?"

Lidia positively hooted at this, attracting bemused glances from the other tables.

"Ya man, Torsten. We is simple folk an' we believe dat ya like who ya like, and if dat be man, woman, or sometin' in between, go for it! We have enough babyfarians runnin' around on dis islan' anyways. Little tykes!" she added, affectionately. "Why, 'as someone caught your eye?" she asked, looking at Torsten mischievously.

"Helvete, no!" said Torsten. "I think my courting days are well and truly over. Anyway, who'd want a wrinkled old sneglhund like me?"

"Oh, ah don' know," twinkled Lidia, "If ya wasn' me cousin an' all …..".

They both collapsed in fits of helpless giggles at this. When Torsten finally recovered, Sophia pulled him up to dance and he found himself caught up in the magical whorl of the music. He felt almost young again.

"I should teach them the Time Warp," he thought, and surrendered himself totally to the irresistible beat.

CHAPTER SIX

The Blomsthilda

The island idyll continued uninterrupted. Surprisingly, the new arrivals didn't miss technology at all, even Haakon, who had spent most of his life in front of a computer screen. He had quickly abandoned his smart suit and was openly embracing the loincloth look. Torsten also needed a change of clothes but balked at the idea of wearing a small piece of fabric around his private parts, despite the fact that he had worn something equally skimpy in his past, theatrical life. He really didn't think he could get away with it now though and, with images of elegant figures from Roman history books in mind, he begged Lidia to have a robe made which looked something along the lines of a toga, and which suited him very well indeed.

One night after dinner, as they were companionably puffing on their pipes, Lidia finally asked Torsten about his family back home, which, by extension, was her family too. He started to explain but then thought it would be easier to draw a family tree. He asked if they had any paper and was given a large piece of parchment, a quill made from the feathers of an indigenous, flightless bird called a miumiu after its haunting call, and a pot of ink made essentially from berries. He wasn't used to writing with a quill, but he did his best and managed to scrawl a reasonable-looking family tree with Bestefar up at the top.

Lidia, Sophia and Penelope were fascinated and read all the names, struggling a little with the pronunciation.

"You remind me of my sister, Dordi," said Torsten to Lidia.

She smiled her toothless smile at him.

"Except for that," he added as an afterthought.

He didn't say this out loud, though.

Torsten felt bad. He hadn't really spared a thought for poor Dordi. He realised now that she was probably worried sick about him, just disappearing like that. They didn't talk much these days, but they spoke on the jellybone every now and then, and she came up to the cottage when she could. Somewhat reluctantly, he realised that he would have to go back home. This proved to be easier said than done, however.

"Do you have any boats at all?" he asked Lidia.

"Nah, man!" replied Lidia. "Ah knows what ya tinkin' ..... pretty strange for folk who live on an islan', right?"

"Yes, a bit," smiled Torsten, "but you already explained why. I just thought maybe you might have one tucked away somewhere for emergencies!"

It was decided that a boat must be built. Nobody knew anything about building boats, but Torsten thought he could cobble together a reasonable raft, with some help from the Bestefarians. A sturdy one should be sufficient to get him safely across the sea back home, he hoped. It would be just him for the return journey, as he had discussed it with Haakon and he had told Torsten in no uncertain terms that there was no way in Helvete that he was going back to Traansylvania. Firstly, because he was unlikely to get a warm welcome, and secondly, he was madly in love with Calypso and had no desire to leave her.

Lidia was confused about the fact that he didn't insist on taking his manservant back with him. Torsten hated lying to Lidia, so he finally confessed that Haakon wasn't really his manservant at all and that he hadn't wanted to say anything at first, but he had done something bad in Traansylvania and couldn't go back. Also, he had not had any problems with Haakon since he arrived on the island and was glad to see that he had found someone to love and who seemed to bring out the best in him.

Tortsten did think, however, that Haakon could spend his time more productively than lying around on the beach waiting for Calypso to finish her chores. Lidia had told Torsten that the village school was desperately short of teachers. It had been set up by Bestefar and Anthe, and she had taught there when he left, followed by her daughter and granddaughter. Sophia was still teaching there, together with Penelope and a handful of other fellow Bestefarians, but there were a lot of children now, and they desperately needed help, so Torsten volunteered Haakon.

He absolutely hated the idea at first, but found, to his surprise, that he actually liked the little ones, and they liked him too. He took them out on hikes and taught them to swim and even play a kind of game of baseball with the hard, round nuts that grew on the trees near the beach. It also helped that it earned him extra kudos with Calypso.

In the meantime, the raft building was not going well. The weather had turned cooler and the days were shorter, meaning that work had to finish earlier. The building team was also learning by trial and error, and several times they had to go back to the drawing board. Only when the warmer days came again did they start making some real progress.

One afternoon, after a marathon morning building session, Torsten had retired to his hut (he was no longer sharing with Haakon, who was now permanently shacked up with Calypso) for a well-earned nap, when he was awoken by shouting from the direction of the beach. He got up to see what all the fuss was about. When he reached the beach, he saw that the entire population of the village seemed to have got there before him. Their turquoise faces were all looking out to sea and they were pointing and chattering excitedly. He pushed his way as best he could through the crowd and found Haakon.

"What's going on?" asked Torsten.

Haakon turned, his face pink with excitement.

"I was doing my afternoon PE class with the kids, and one of them saw something out at sea. I thought he was imagining things at first, but then we all saw it …. it's a boat!"

Torsten followed his pointing finger out to sea and, indeed, he could see a vague dot on the horizon. He saw Lidia and Sophia nearby.

As he approached them, he could hear Lidia saying in urgent tones, "We should soun' da alarm. It time for Operation Scare'emoff!"

She was about to give the order when Torsten suddenly cried out, "Wait, it's the Blomsthilda!"

He could hardly believe his eyes. It looked, from a distance, very like Bestefar's magnificent, old sailing boat; he remembered it so well from when he was a boy. But he thought that Bestefar had sold it after Torsten's parents were lost at sea with their boat. In his grief, Bestefar had declared that he had no wish to sail any more. And yet, as it approached the shore, he could now clearly see the two proud masts with the sails furled and could even make out the sky-blue colour of the hull.

"Da Blomsthilda," repeated Lidia. "What dat?"

"It's Bestefar's boat," said Torsten.

Lidia looked surprised but dismissed the men waiting around her to sound the alarm with a wave of her hand.

"Are ya sure 'bout dis, Mamma?" asked Sophia nervously.

Lidia nodded.

"If Torsten say it Bestefar boat, den I trust 'im." She turned to Torsten, "Surely den, it mus' be family if it really his."

"Well, yes," replied Torsten, slightly yellow-tinged with worry, "but I didn't think Bestefar had kept it."

"Ah was tinkin' mebbe someone come lookin' for ya sooner or later, Torsten man," said Lidia.

By this time, the boat had stopped a way out from the beach and Torsten could clearly see two figures on board frantically waving, but it was impossible at that distance to see who they were. Before long, a rowing boat came into view and both Torsten and Haakon were flabbergasted to see who was straining at the oars.

"Holy dritt," said Torsten. "It's BJ!"

"Holy dritt," said Haakon almost simultaneously. "It's Freki!"

He didn't seem over the moons to see either of them.

"Who is it?" asked Lidia. "Friend or foe?"

"Depends on your point of view," replied Torsten cheerfully.

He, for one, was delighted at this turn of events. Particularly since it meant he probably wouldn't have to brave the ocean on the still-far-from-robust raft that was a work in progress. Lidia looked perplexed.

"It's my great-nephew, BJ … Patrik … named after Bestefar actually. And his friend, Freki."

"Freki," repeated Lidia.

"Yes, I know," sighed Torsten.

He waded out into the surf to greet the two men and help them drag the rowing boat up onto the shore.

BJ and Freki both gave Torsten a huge hug and he hugged them both back warmly. They turned to Haakon who was hanging back looking sheepish.

"You're still alive then?" said BJ, with about as much warmth as a polar ice cap.

Haakon shrugged.

More such niceties were prevented by the arrival of Lidia, Sophia and Penelope, who had also come to see who these mysterious strangers might be. The other Bestefarians were also starting to crowd around the new arrivals and the two men were starting to look slightly panic-stricken, so Lidia intervened.

"Dis is Bestefar's great-great-grandson and 'is manservant (this was becoming quite a thing, it seemed)," she declaimed to the assembled throng, who backed away respectfully.

"Leave us now," she continued, "Bestefar be wid y'all!"

This was greeted with a general cry of "Ya, man," and the crowds began to disperse.

Lidia smiled her best, benign, toothless smile on those who remained on the beach and said to Torsten, "Come, we leave ya to catch up wid your family. We catch ya later at dinner, alright?"

Torsten nodded and the last of the Bestefarian contingent drifted back towards the village. Haakon got his diminutive charges lined up and began marching them off in the same direction.

Freki called out, "Like the loincloth, man!"

Haakon didn't react and continued his dogged march.

"So?" said Torsten to BJ once they were alone.

"Aunty Dordi sent us," BJ said. "She was worried about you, and Petra was feeling kind of bad about what she did to Haakon too, so they sent us on a mission to find you both. We had to wait a while, of course, assuming that you'd gone back in time and blah blah blah blah ... you know."

"How did Dordi know I'd be here," asked Torsten. "She couldn't possibly know, unless ...."

An unpleasant thought popped into his brain and decided it quite liked it there and might stay awhile.

"Why don't you just ask her?" said BJ pragmatically.

He pulled a mobile phone out of his pocket and pressed a key.

"We're here," he said to the screen and passed it over to Torsten.

Dordi's face appeared, yellowish-grey and looking older than Torsten remembered.

"Torsten," the face said, "thank Odin you're alright."

"Dordi," said Torsten. "It's good to see you, but what the …..? And what's with the Blomsthilda?"

"I can explain," said Dordi breathlessly. "Well, Bestefar can explain … not in person, obviously … BJ has something with him that will tell you everything you need to know. I'm so sorry, Torsten, but he swore me to secrecy. I didn't know what to do … forgive me!"

She burst into tears and Torsten's heart twisted in his chest.

"It's alright, sis," he said, more kindly. "We'll sort this out. Talk to you later?"

Dordi nodded wordlessly and the screen went blank. Torsten handed the phone back to BJ.

"So where's this something that will explain everything then?" he asked.

BJ produced a notebook from a rather battered, old leather satchel he'd been carrying over his shoulder. The notebook, like the satchel, looked like it had seen better days.

"Isn't that …?" said Torsten.

"Petra senior's? Yeah," replied BJ with the ghost of a smile. "My sister insisted I bring it along for good luck, the silly sneglhund."

"Have you read it?" asked Torsten, taking the notebook from BJ.

BJ nodded. Freki was studying the sand at his feet as if it were doing something interesting.

"Okay," said Torsten.

He looked a little lost for a moment, gazing out at the Blomsthilda, but then he rallied, clapped BJ on the back and said, "Let's go and find Lidia. I'm sure she's already got a hut ready for you both. I need to do a bit of reading, it would appear."

They walked together through the trees to the village. Lidia was nowhere to be seen, but her favourite manservant was waiting to escort BJ and Freki to a hut to rest after their journey.

Torsten took his leave and walked purposefully to his hut, clutching the notebook, his head reeling. He sat down heavily on his pallet and opened the notebook to the first page. He recognised Bestefar's slanted script immediately.

"My dear Torsten," he read.

CHAPTER SEVEN

A voice from beyond the grave

My dear Torsten,

If you are reading this, then I am dead and you have been to the Otherland and found out certain things about me that I'm sure will have shocked you.

I always knew that the truth would come out one day, and now I am old and sense that the end is near, I have told Dordi everything and will ask her to keep this letter hidden away until such time as you need to read it.

I'd better start from the very beginning. Seems like a good place to start.

There's that song again, thought Torsten. He shook his head to clear it and continued reading.

It was the month of Sólmánudr, many, many moons ago. I had just completed my studies and was longing for some adventure. I was courting your Bestemor at the time, but didn't feel ready to settle down just yet. Coward that I was, I was afraid of what she might say if I told her, so I left her a note and sailed off one morning in my parents' boat. I had always been fascinated by the Otherland. We were taught at school that it was an awful, lawless place, overrun with mindless savages. It was written in Baldursson's Lore that He had sent emissaries there long ago to spread His Word, but that one of them was eaten and the other barely made it back alive to tell the tale. With all the foolish arrogance of youth, I set sail for this isle of iniquity and found, to my surprise and delight, that the inhabitants were more than welcoming, although they spoke in a language incomprehensible to me. And there I met the other love of my life, Anthe.

Her parents were originally from the Otherland, but it seems that there are islands even beyond, inhabited by strange and powerful beings, who have kidnapped Otherlanders in the past and made them their slaves. Anthe's father had been unjustly accused of stealing and, to avoid the death sentence hanging over him, he took his wife and child and a small boat and they made the treacherous crossing over the Odd Sea to the Otherland, where they found refuge.

The Theoi, which is apparently the name of these overlords, are able to make the crossing without difficulty as they are masters also of the Nereides: fair but frightening creatures who can control the sea and all of the beasts that live within it, compelling them to terrorise unsuspecting travellers. They themselves would often sit preening themselves on rocky outcrops, combing their long locks and singing songs so heart-achingly beautiful that no sailor could resist. They would be drawn to the haunting sound and dashed to their deaths against the treacherous rocks.

Anthe, however, had befriended some of the odd sea creatures and swam with them often. As she and her parents began the perilous crossing, they recognised their friend and protected her from harm. They arrived safely back on the shores of their home, were welcomed back as heroes and had managed to bring some measure of civilisation to their people even before I arrived on the scene.

Anthe means 'flower' in her language, but she was more beautiful and beguiling than any flower. We couldn't speak each other's languages at first, but we still seemed to understand one another just fine. We invented a language of our own. Time seemed meaningless and I was so happy helping her teach the Otherlanders and watch them become the people they are, I assume, still today. They loved us; venerated us even. I knew how Baldursson must have felt.

Then, one night, I had a dream about Hilda, your Bestemor. She was in the sea, fighting some terrible creature that was trying to devour her. She kept screaming and disappearing beneath the waves and then she would reappear briefly, desperately crying out my name over and over. It was so vivid. I awoke in a cold sweat and Anthe was stroking my brow. She asked me what dream could trouble me so and I broke down and told her the truth. She sent me away then, saying that I could not break a promise already made to another, but I would have gone anyway, knowing in my heart of hearts that she was right. It took all my strength to wrench myself

away, however, and I was sick in my heart and body as I sailed back to
Traansylvania.

Hilda was touchingly pleased to see me and I her. I never told her where
I'd been and she carefully never asked. I begged her pardon for my abrupt
departure and long absence and she very kindly bestowed it upon me. We
were married shortly after. When my parents passed away, I renamed
their boat 'Blomsthilda' in honour of my two loves (I couldn't name Anthe,
of course, so I translated her name), and Hilda liked it. She thought I was
comparing her to a flower, so I let her believe that.

As you know, when your parents died at sea, I couldn't bear to sail any
more and wouldn't let you and Dordi either. But I also couldn't bear to part
with the Blomsthilda, so I hid her away in a secret mooring.

I was heartbroken when your Bestemor passed away. We had a long and
happy life together and I loved her very much. I grew weary of rattling
about in the cottage by myself and busied myself with my historical
research. I got very enthusiastic over my project to write an updated
biography of Baldursson. I found out incidentally that he had indeed sent
emissaries in the past to the Otherland to explore. None of them was eaten
and they came back and reported that it was just an island full of primitive
people who represented no real threat but also no real interest. Baldursson
left it at that.

I was to begin writing, as you know, when you came to my cottage a few
years back and announced that you were all going to visit Baldursson in

the past. I was sorely tempted to come with you, but when Petra explained her incredible invention to me, it gave me an idea. I was already too old to sail the Blomsthilda across to the Otherland, but I wanted so badly to go and see Anthe once more that I secretly begged Petra to give me that possibility.

She didn't ask any questions, but gave me the bracelet and the black box, set the coordinates and, as soon as you had all gone to the Traansylvania of the past, I pressed that button. Sadly, I was too late, and my poor old heart was broken once more. I had the joy, however, of finding out that I was a father and a grandfather all over again. Eleftheria (Anthe called her that because it means 'freedom' in her language, as she was the first child born out of slavery), my Otherland daughter, was furious with me at first, and rightfully so, but she generously forgave me. Her daughter Lidia was a bright, pretty young thing and reminded me of darling Dordi. Once again, however, I felt compelled to return to Traansylvania and be the best Bestefar I could to you both.

You are probably wondering why I have not told you any of this before. I was quite simply ashamed of my guilty secret and did not want you or Dordi to think badly of me. And Please do not blame her for not telling you. I swore the poor child to secrecy. I also showed her where the Blomsthilda was hidden so you can decide whether you wish to keep her. I hope you do. I also asked Dordi to bury the magic bracelet with me so that there was no possibility it would fall into the wrong hands.

So there you have it, my beloved Barnebarn. Now you know everything. I hope you can find it in your heart to forgive me as Dordi has, and also that if you have met your family in the

Otherland, you will love them as much as I did, and as much as I love you and your sister. Take good care of each other.

Your Bestefar

CHAPTER EIGHT

Dordi's despair

Dordi awoke feeling old.

"Well, I am old," she said to herself reasonably as she looked at her reflection in the bathroom mirror.

She was also feeling anxious. She had tried to call Torsten the night before to see if he wanted to come and see Annette, Petra and Sander's little one and the newest member of the family, as Petra didn't want to travel yet with a newborn. Unusually, there had been no reply. Dordi worried about Torsten, pottering about alone in Bestefar's cottage with only his grief for company.

She wasn't hungry, so she made Arne some breakfast and then tried Torsten again. Still no reply. She tried one more time after lunch and, now seriously concerned, called her daughter and asked her to look after Arne while she drove up to the cottage by the sea. Elea wanted to go with her, but Dordi said that she wanted to go alone as she needed to talk to her brother about something important.

She had been thinking more and more about what Bestefar had confided to her before he died. The burden of it had been weighing on her unbearably recently and she had already decided to tell Torsten the next time she saw him. She rehearsed what she was going to say as she drove.

She arrived at the cottage in the late afternoon. The warm, salty air assailed her nose holes as she got out of the car and a hundred thousand memories assailed her mind as she walked towards the familiar front door. She knocked, but there was no sound other than the crashing of the waves and the cawing of the gulls. She tried the door. It was open, so she stepped inside and called Torsten's name. Still nothing, so she searched the cottage from top to bottom. No Torsten. The only signs of his having been there were an unmade bed, an empty tea cup by the sink and an open cupboard in the library with a box on the floor nearby.

She went outside into the garden. From there, she could just about make out the clifftop temple and wondered if Torsten had gone up to his favourite vantage point. She walked laboriously up the hill to the bench, but it was empty. She tried the temple, but it was dark and empty likewise. Finally, she reached the graveyard and there, a dreadful sight awaited her. Bestefar's headstone was rent right down the middle and his grave was open as if the earth had been ripped aside by some infernal, deranged creature. The coffin was visible and the lid had been pushed aside by the force of whatever had wreaked this havoc. Horrified, she could just make out Bestefar's bones beneath the earth that had fallen into the coffin, and, like a beacon, the stone on the bracelet shimmering eerily in the light of the setting sun.

Dordi reeled back. Her first thought was that it might have been grave robbers, but that would not explain Torsten's mysterious disappearance. She staggered back up to the bench and sat, breathing heavily and trying to gather her thoughts. She remembered the open cupboard in the library and the box. She remembered the bracelet still attached to Bestefar's bony wrist and shuddered. She had a horrible feeling she knew what had happened to her brother.

It was getting dark and she had no wish to remain in this profaned place any longer. She drove home as fast as she could and even though she was emotionally and physically drained, she asked Elea to call an emergency family conference.

They all came straight over despite the late hour, a sleeping Annette cuddled up to Petra in a sling, and Dordi told them everything. Arne, who was sitting in an armchair wrapped up in a blanket, began to chuckle.

"Bestefar, you old sneglhund," he wheezed. "Always knew there was more to you than met the eyes."

He became serious again when he saw the look on Dordi's face.

"So what do you think happened to Torsten then?" he asked.

"Well, it's obvious," said Petra. "He found the console, and the bracelet Bestefar was buried with triggered a massive energy vortex, which Torsten got caught up in."

Arne nodded dumbly.

"Is that even possible?" asked Sander, taken aback.

"It is possible," said Elea. "Freakishly unlikely, but possible."

"So he's been transported somewhere?" said Dordi, hovering halfway between relief at knowing he was alive and horror at how far he may have travelled and in which direction.

Arne could feel one of his old migraines coming on and Elea quickly gave him an injection of painkillers. He asked meekly for a glass of brannenmjød and Dordi obliged, given the circumstances.

Coming back to her question, she asked her granddaughter's opinion, as she was more familiar with Petra senior's technology.

"Two possible options," said Petra. "Either he's been sent back to the faraway past when Bestefar visited the Otherland, or he's been sent back to the recent past following the energy signal I used to banish Haakon. Either way, he's in the Otherland. Probably," she added, as her Oldemor had taught her that good scientists always leave a margin for experimental error.

"So we can get him back then?" asked Dordi weakly.

"We can't go back in time," said Petra. "But if he *has* been transported to the instant when Haakon arrived in the Otherland, we will have to wait six months or so for time to catch up with us."

Arne groaned into his brannenmjød, making bubbles.

"That'll give us time to get the Blomsthilda shipshape again," said Dordi. "I went to see her and she's in a bit of a bad way."

"But who will sail her?" asked Sander. "Do any of you know how to sail?"

"I did," said Dordi quietly.

"I'll do it," said BJ. "I'm the boss of my own company, so I'll take some time off, and I reckon I could learn how to sail in six months. I already know a bit about it."

"But you can't manage the Blomsthilda by yourself," said Dordi, "You'd need somebody with you."

"I'll take Freki," said BJ breezily. "It'll be like a road trip but on the sea."

"Maybe I should go," offered Jan bravely. "You might need help with those savages."

Elea shook her head and looked worried.

"Do you really believe those stories?" she asked.

"No," said Jan, but he didn't look convinced.

"It's okay," said Dordi, smiling for the first time that day. She told them what Bestefar had said in his letter about the Otherlanders.

"That's settled then," said BJ. "I'll speak to Freki tomorrow and tell him to get tacking."

It was a sailing joke and only Dordi actually got it. She smiled again and breathed a sigh of relief.

"Hang in there, brother," she said to herself. "You're in for a big surprise."

CHAPTER NINE

Love is in the air

Torsten closed the notebook and leaned back on his pallet, closing his eyes, which were wet with tears. Even though Bestefar was long gone, he felt closer to him now than ever. He felt sorry that this wise, kind, gentle man had felt he had to keep this secret all those years. He lay for a while in the gathering darkness, mulling over what he had read.

He was interrupted by a knock at the door of his hut. One of Lidia's manservants appeared with BJ and Freki in tow.

"Dese gentlemen was a-lookin' for ya, Mista Torsten," he said with a slight bow.

Torsten sighed. He had tried many times to stop the servants from calling him "Mista", to no avail.

Torsten thanked him and he bowed again and left. BJ and Freki were both glowing pale in the half-light.

"Are you alright, Uncle T?" asked BJ. "Did you read the letter?"

"Yes," replied Torsten. "Don't worry, BJ. Everything's fine."

The two young men looked relieved.

"Can you please tell Aunty D that?" said BJ. "She's been messaging me constantly to find out how you took the news?"

Torsten nodded. BJ pressed a key on his phone, passed it to Torsten and once more, Dordi's worried face appeared.

"It's alright, sis," said Torsten. "I understand."

Dordi looked like she was about to cry.

"It's cool, Mrs G," said Freki over Torsten's shoulder.

He liked Dordi. Dordi smiled.

"How's Haakon the Horrible?" she asked.

"Behaving himself," replied Torsten, smiling back. "For now. He's in lurve."

"Oh," said Dordi, surprised. "Who with? Himself?"

BJ and Freki snorted.

"Ha ha," said Torsten. "No, actually, with a rather pretty servant girl. Calypso. She's been good for him. And believe it or not, he's now a PE teacher at the village school."

"Wonders will never cease," said Dordi "And you?"

"I'm not a PE teacher, and I'm not in love, but I'm fine," said Torsten, and he meant it.

"I'd almost finished building a raft to travel back, but you saved me the trouble by sending the boys."

Dordi looked amused.

"I didn't know you could build rafts."

"I can't," replied Torsten. "That's why it's taken so long!"

Dordi laughed.

"So what happens now?" she asked. "Are you coming home?"

"Wouldn't you like to come here?" asked Torsten "Meet the family? The boys could hop over and pick you up in the Blomsthilda."

He did his familiar jazz hands thing. There was a pause.

"I'd like to," said Dordi hesitantly, "really, I would. But Arne's not well, Torsten. I can't leave him. He sends his love, by the way."

Torsten felt a lump rise in his throat. He was inordinately fond of his brother-in-law.

"The kids are fine, though," said Dordi, perking up. "They all say hi too."

"Give them all huge hugs from me," said Torsten. "We'll have a family conference over here and let you know what we decide to do."

"Alright," said Dordi. "And get BJ to send pictures. And your mother says to call her every day, BJ … you hear?"

"Yes Aunty," said BJ with mock weariness.

They all waved at Dordi and the screen went blank.

"Shall we go and see if dinner's ready?" said Torsten. "I'm so hungry I could eat a whole ullabeist!"

"A what?" said BJ and Freki in unison.

"You'll see," said Torsten and led the way to the warm and welcoming dining area.

People were milling about, drinking and chatting. A loinclothed servant brought them some cups on a tray and BJ and Freki sipped the wine appreciatively.

"I'm feeling a bit overdressed," said BJ, looking at the servant, even though he and Freki were dressed only in shorts and t-shirts.

He was about to say something else, but his eye was caught by a willowy serving girl passing by with a basket of bread. He looked at Freki and whistled through his teeth.

"And how is Lise these days?" asked Torsten meaningfully.

BJ and Lise Lauritsen, the well-known journalist, had been dating for a while now. They were quite the celebrity couple.

"Ah… erm … she's fine," replied BJ and applied himself to drinking his wine.

"What's with the hats, man?" asked Freki, still looking around.

"These people are Bestefarians," said Torsten.

BJ and Freki looked puzzled.

"When Bestefar came the first time, he left his sailing hat behind, and then after he left the second time, he became a cult figure and everyone wears the hats in his honour," Torsten explained.

"Wow," said BJ.

"Cool," said Freki. "Where can I get one?"

Lidia and Sophia suddenly appeared out of the throng and Torsten made formal introductions. Lidia was thrilled.

"Ah can' believe we got ourselves a baby Bestefar right 'ere, now man!" she said, enveloping BJ in a huge hug and planting a huge, wet kiss on his pinky-grey cheek.

BJ did what every child who gets kissed by an elderly aunt does and wiped it off with the back of his hand. Luckily, Lidia didn't notice as she had turned her attention to Freki.

"An' dis den young Freki," she said. "Fine lookin' boy, but funny ol' name."

Freki grinned widely. He was used to people being fazed by his name, but it was not often that he was praised for his looks.

"Can I have a hat?" he asked.

"Ya, man!" cried Lidia, beaming now. "Sophia, mek sure dat after dinner, we present da sacred hats to everybody. We all Bestafarian now. One, big, happy family!"

Sophia smiled and nodded and they moved towards their table, where Penelope was sitting in her usual spot. She got up as they approached. Freki took one look at her and his face transformed into a stroboscopic, spectroscopic sensation: a kaleidoscopic cacophony of colour both amusing and confusing. At the same time, his mouth was opening and closing like a dying goldfish and he finally managed to say something that sounded very much like "meep".

Penelope just smiled and patted the chair beside her, inviting Freki to sit down. Freki looked at BJ in a blind panic. His face had finally settled into a kind of graduated ripple of green, turquoise, yellow, grey and pink. BJ nodded and smiled and Freki sat down gingerly and started nervously playing with a piece of bread whilst everyone else took their seats.

Torsten told Lidia, Sophia and Penelope about the letter and his conversation with Dordi.

"Ah don' understan'," said Lidia. "What dis ting you can talk to Dordi wid over da sea? How dis possible? Bestefar had no such ting when he cum 'ere."

"It's called technology," said Torsten. "And the ting ...err ... thing we use to talk to each other is called a jellybone, although Petra likes to call it a 'mobile'."

He gestured to BJ to give him the phone and he passed it to Lidia.

She took it carefully as if it were going to bite her and then held it up in front of her and intoned, "O great Jellybone. Ah wish to talk to Dordi o' Traansylvania."

The Traansylvanians chuckled.

"It doesn't work like that," said Torsten kindly, taking the device from Lidia.

He pushed a key, there was a brief vibration and then Dordi appeared. She looked flustered.

"By da light o' da moons, girl," exclaimed Lidia, "why ya so white like a ghost?"

"Hello to you too," said Dordi, surprised at seeing a face that looked a lot like hers on the screen in front of her.

"Dordi, this is Lidia … and Sophia … and Penelope," said Torsten as they all crowded round to wave at Dordi.

"Why *are* you so pale, sis?" he asked, and then a sudden thought struck him.

"It's not Arne, is it?" he asked, yellow-tinged with worry.

"No, no," laughed the pale apparition. "I'm making dumplings and little Annette is helping me."

She turned her phone around to show a smiling Petra holding a bonny baby girl on the flour-covered counter. The child was also covered in flour and was happily dipping her chubby little hands in it and throwing it around the kitchen, gurgling with pleasure.

There was a collective "aaaaah" from the other end of the phone.

"That's Annette," said Torsten. "Petra junior and Sander's little one."

"Hi, Uncle T," said Petra, waving a flour-covered hand. "And newly discovered island family," she added.

They all waved at Petra.

"Hey Pet," said BJ. "How's my little Annetty-Wetty? Say hello to Uncle Patty."

Torsten looked at him as if seeing him for the first time. He didn't know BJ had such a soft side. Petra laughed and took Annette's arm, waving it at BJ.

"I had to tell them," said Dordi to Torsten. "They were all worried sick about you."

"It's ok, Dordi," said Torsten. "Anyway, we have to go. Dinner's ready. Enjoy your dumplings!"

He pressed a key and passed the phone back to BJ.

During dinner, which was delicious, BJ watched Freki giving Penelope furtive looks. If she looked at him, he would quickly look away. BJ found this highly amusing.

After dinner, the traditional kaya pipes came out and Torsten explained what it was and how nice and relaxed it made you feel.

"Looks like Freki could do with some," he remarked. "He's as nervous as a sneglkattunge!"

Torsten let Lidia, Sophia and Penelope read Bestefar's letter. Penelope handed the notebook reverently back to Torsten. They were all silent for a while, puffing on their pipes. The hypnotic music had started up again and they were all bobbing their heads along to the beat. Freki had his eyes closed and appeared to be in a trance.

"Lidia, did your Bestemor say anything about the other place where she lived as a child and where her parents were enslaved?" he eventually asked.

"She didn' say much," replied Lidia. "Ah don' tink she liked to talk about it. She jus' said dat deir masters was fearsome powerful folk."

"Did they say what the place was called?" asked BJ, still watching Freki out of the corner of his eyes.

"Ah don' recall rightly," answered Lidia. "But ah tink it sounded sometin' like Limp Puss."

Freki's eyes snapped open.

"Limp Puss," he snorted.

"Like a flat katt!" BJ giggled and slapped his friend so hard on the back he almost fell off his chair.

Penelope caught Freki and dragged him off to dance. Everyone watched them for a while. BJ nodded along to the music approvingly.

Torsten continued with his train of thought, chuffing along, emitting kaya-scented smoke.

"And you say these beings kidnapped Otherlanders and made them their slaves?"

"Ya, man," Lidia nodded vigorously. "Dey haven' come for long, long time now, though. Metink mebbe dey don' need no more slaves."

Torsten nodded.

"And if they did come?" he asked.

"We cross dat sea when we comes to it," said Lidia.

BJ wasn't listening any more. He couldn't quite believe his eyes. It might have been a kaya-induced hallucination, but he appeared to be watching his best friend walk hand in hand into the sunset with the most beautiful girl on the island.

CHAPTER TEN

A visitation

They all drifted off to bed, the Traansylvanians clutching their new Bestefarian hats, presented to them by Lidia with great ceremony, except for Freki, who had disappeared off in the direction of the beach with Penelope. BJ was carrying his and wearing his own.

The next day, they reconvened at noon, wearing their hats. Torsten was finding it difficult to get used to and the ullabeist wool made his head itch. He missed the light panama hat Kim had bought him and which he had been obliged to leave behind at Misselthwaite. Freki turned up late, grinning from ear hole to ear hole.

They discussed what they wanted to do. Torsten wanted to go back to Traansylvania as he was worried about Arne and Dordi. BJ expressed a strong interest in sailing over to Limp Puss and giving the inhabitants a piece of his mind about the evils of slavery. Nobody else seemed thrilled at the prospect. Haakon was at school and didn't get a vote anyway.

"I wanna stay here," said Freki.

"Well, that's a big surprise," said BJ.

"Oh, come on, man," said Freki. "This is the best thing that's ever happened to me, like, ever!"

"Well, I can't sail the Blomsthilda by myself," said Torsten.

"Why don't you ask the Bestefarians to go with you?" asked BJ.

Given what Lidia had said, Torsten didn't think they'd want to go, and anyway, none of them had any sailing experience.

"Don't you want to go back and see Lise?" Torsten asked BJ.

BJ looked uncomfortable.

"Well, yeah …," he said, "but honestly, she's quite high maintenance, and I could do with a holiday."

"Me too, man," said Freki with feeling. "My boss is, like, a bit of a tyrant, in spite of his strong, anti-slavery opinions."

BJ rolled his eyes and Torsten laughed.

"Alright, alright, I suppose another week or so won't do any harm," he said.

BJ messaged his mother and told her they'd decided to stay for a while. She told him to make sure he changed his underwear every day, to which he replied that Bestefarians didn't wear underwear.

Torsten and Sophia enjoyed showing BJ and Freki around the island, and Penelope now almost always accompanied them on their walks. They were also back on speaking terms with Haakon, who they invariably bumped into every now and then as it wasn't a large island.

And so time passed pleasantly, and much more than a week had gone by when something happened to disturb the harmony of the happy holiday-makers and the quiet life of the island in general.

They awoke one morning to find the village in an uproar. The dinner gong was clashing the alarm call, everyone was running about in a panic and Lidia was trying her best to calm everyone.

"What's happened?" asked Torsten, finally managing to push through the jostling, agitated crowd with BJ and Freki close behind.

"Dey came!" said Lidia, choking out the words, obviously very distressed. "Dey came durin' da night an' took some of our young ones."

She seemed to crumple before their very eyes, and Sophia and Penelope, on either side of her, supported her and sat her down in a chair.

Haakon came running up to them, out of breath and red in the face.

"They've taken Calypso!" he shouted.

He was wide-eyed and livid and Torsten imagined that if he had any hair, he would be pulling it out right about now.

"Dey only took servants," Sophia explained. "Da one whose huts was closes' to da beach."

"Ah never tought dis day achally come," wailed Lidia. "Oh what are we to do?"

"Well, I'm going over there," announced Haakon, climbing onto one of the wooden tables. "I'm going to get her back. Who's with me?"

There was a sudden, uncomfortable silence.

"Well?" roared Haakon. "What are you? Men or mus?"

Lidia stood up shakily and leaned on her stick.

"You 'ave no idea what ya dealin' wid, man," she said. "Dese no or'nary people. My Bestemor said dat dey magical creature; some o' dem kill ya wid a single glance.

Metink even our strongest warriors not stand a chance, and don' forget no-one manage to cross da Odd Sea alive, 'cept my Bestemor."

"I don't care," said Haakon. "I'm still going and I'll go alone if I have to. Torsten, I commandeer the Blosmthilda."

"Wha ....., wait," spluttered Torsten,. "You can't!"

"We needs to hol' a crisis meetin' right now," said Lidia firmly. "Haakon, get yersel' down from dere and stop yer rantin'. Everyone, go back to your business for now while we decide what best to do. Bestefar be wid y'all."

"Ya, man," came the response and everyone dutifully left, apart from Lidia, Sophia, Penelope, the Traansylvanians and Lidia's most trusted manservant, whose name was Ganymede.

They sat around a table and Lidia sent Ganymede to fetch wine. Haakon was still agitated and was drumming his fingers impatiently on the table. Lidia shot him a look, and he stopped.

"You can't stop me going," he said.

"We can if we take the Blomsthilda back home," retorted BJ.

"You wouldn't!" shouted Haakon.

"Watch me!" shouted back BJ.

"Hey, cool it guys," said Freki.

"Stop yer hollerin'!" shouted Lidia, almost causing Ganymede to drop the tray of wine cups he was carefully carrying towards them. "We need to tink about dis calmly and rationally now."

She took out her clay pipe and told Ganymede to bring a pot of fresh kaya, which he promptly did.

"So you're just going to sit around smoking, are you?" seethed Haakon, barely able to contain his frustration.

"Ya, man," responded Lidia, waving her pipe at him, "an' mebbe you should 'ave a pipeful too. Calm ya down a bit."

"Don't you care about Calypso and the others?" asked Haakon, but he took some kaya anyway and started angrily stuffing his pipe with it.

"O' course ah do," retorted Lidia as Ganymede lit her pipe. "Whaddaya take me for? But it seem impossible to cross da Odd Sea, and even more impossible to get dem back from da Theoi. Watcha gonna do? Shout 'em to death?"

"Is it impossible, though?" asked Torsten thoughtfully. "Anthe and her parents made it across."

"True dat," nodded Lidia and took a good slug of wine.

Haakon had calmed down considerably and was now looking at Lidia with something like hope shining in his eyes, pupils wildly dilated from the kaya.

"If we did manage to get across," he said, "I'd be willing to brave whatever dangers. Do whatever it takes. I don't care how magical or powerful they are."

"Ya really do love dat girl, dontcha?" asked Lidia.

Haakon nodded. Everyone looked at Lidia expectantly and she looked at Sophia.

"What ya tinkin', daughter?" she asked.

Sophia puffed thoughtfully on her pipe for a moment and said, "Well, Mamma, dere always da song, ya know."

"Aaaaah, da song," said Lidia.

"What song?" said Haakon quickly, beating the others to it.

"Da siren song dat Bestemor sing to my mamma, an' dat she sing to me, an' dat I sing to you, Sophia," said Lidia softly.

"And dat Mamma sing to me," murmured Penelope. "Is dat a real siren song, den? I always tought it was jus' a made-up ting."

"Bestemor said so," replied Lidia. "Dat all ah know."

Freki looked at Penelope and then at Haakon.

"I'd die if you were taken away from me," he said, taking her hand. "We should try to help Calypso and the others."

Penelope sighed, breathing out kaya smoke through her nose holes like an elegant dragon.

"If *you* come wid me, ah try it," she said to Freki.

They all made as if to get up, but Penelope gestured for them to stop.

"Only Freki," she said.

She kissed her mother and Lidia, took Freki by the hand and they left, Freki grabbing a fresh bread roll from the table as he passed. Nobody apart from Freki felt like eating. They sat mostly in silence, sipping wine and smoking kaya.

They returned in the early afternoon. Everyone was still sitting where they had left them and they had only picked at their lunch.

"Cool," said Freki, flopping down into a chair. "Lunch. I'm starving!"

He looked up from his food when he realised everyone was looking at him expectantly.

"What?" he mumbled through a mouthful of ullabeist stew. "Have I got something on my face?"

Penelope put her hands on his shoulders from behind and everyone looked at her instead. She nodded and smiled and sat down next to Freki. She looked tired.

"Yes!" cried Haakon and punched the air with his fist. "Let's go then!"

"Hold your ullabeistene, Haakon, man," said Lidia. "We haven' decided if we goin' yet."

She looked at Penelope "So da song work den?"

Penelope said, "Like a charm, Mormor. It was scary at firs', but den it was jus'… magical."

"It was pretty cool," agreed Freki, helping himself to another bowl of stew and serving some for Penelope. "All that walking's given me an appetite."

"So I see," said BJ drily, but he was pleased to see his friend back safe and sound.

"So are we going then?" said Haakon, his already limited supply of patience rapidly running out.

Lidia spoke.

"Well, ah's too ol' to be gallivantin' round da place."

Oh how she resembled Bestefar, thought Torsten.

"But if anyone be brave or stupid enough to go (she was looking straight at Haakon at this point), ah won' stop dem."

"I'll go," Penelope said, a cupful of wine giving her courage.

"If she goes, I go," said Freki.

"If Freki goes, I go," said BJ.

Lidia looked at Sophia.

She shook her head and said, "Someone need to stay and look after da school. An' you, Mamma."

Everyone looked at Torsten, who had gone a sickly shade of yellow.

"Well," he said eventually, "someone needs to keep an eye or two on you lot. So, one for all, and all for one!"

"Ah take it dat mean yes?" said Lidia, her face crinkled in a smile.

Torsten nodded. The others whooped and Lidia made an announcement to the villagers and a toast to safe travels.

Haakon was all for leaving straight away, but they were all tired at this point after the day's emotions and Penelope looked like she was fit to drop. Torsten told them it would be better to wait for the morning tide, so they all retired to their huts to prepare for the journey and get some rest.

They all called their nearest and dearest to tell them the news. Torsten called Dordi and spoke to Arne too.

"So let me get this straight," wheezed Arne. "You're crossing a sea full of strange, scary, mystical creatures to an island full of strange, scary, mystical creatures to rescue some servants."

"Yup," said Torsten.

"Are any of your island friends going with you?" he asked.

"Penelope, yes," replied Torsten "She's going to sing the siren song."

"Right," said Arne.

"Lidia offered to send some of her people, but we can't fit that many on the boat, and anyway, most of them are terrified about crossing the Odd Sea. It's always been taboo."

"Right," said Arne. "And why are *you* going again?"

Torsten thought about this. He thought about how miserable he had been lately and how quiet and dull his life had become.

"Arne, my old friend," he said, "I'm going on an adventure!"

End of Part I

PART II

An Epic Adventure

Let us prepare to grapple with the ineffable itself, and see if we may not eff it after all.
— Douglas Adams

CHAPTER ONE

The Odd Sea

Despite the earliness of the hour, the entire island seemed to have turned out to see off the rescue party; an unlikely band of heroes if ever there was one. They stood, bleary-eyed and nervous, on the shore beside the rowing boat, with the sun just peeping over the horizon behind them. Only the sound of the lapping waves and the plaintive call of a miumiu somewhere in the trees beyond the beach broke the silence, heavy with expectation.

Lidia, eyes shining, approached and hugged each of them in turn, closely followed by Sophia, holding Penelope in a lingering embrace, unwilling to let her go.

"May Bestefar be wid ya, an' bring ya back safely to us wid our missin' Bestebarns," she said.

"Ya, man," intoned the waiting throng.

Torsten took this as his cue, signalling to the others to push the rowing boat out into the surf. Only when the anchor was weighed and the sails unfurled on the Blomsthilda did they look back to see a vague sea of waving hands on the now-distant beach.

"Here goes nothing," said Torsten, trying to sound braver than he felt, and doing his old jazz hands thing to try to lighten the mood, which was currently heavier than an iridium-clad elephant.

Unsurprisingly, nobody joined in. Haakon was standing at the prow looking stern, and Freki and Penelope were holding hands, appropriately, at the stern, watching the receding shore and the Bestefarians, now reduced to tiny specks in the growing light.

BJ was at the helm. He turned towards Torsten as they approached the headland at the north of the island, where they would turn due west to meet the boundary of the Odd Sea.

"One thing I don't get," he said, turning the wheel to avoid the rocky outcrops jutting from the headland. "Why does the Odd Sea end abruptly at the Otherland?"

Torsten shrugged and Penelope, who was moving with uncanny grace towards them, said, "Ah'm tinkin' dat de Theoi's powers mebbe don' extend so far beyon' deir islan', or perhaps dey jus' need ta protec' dat part o' da sea dat separate deir island from ours."

Torsten nodded.

"Dat … I mean … *that* would make sense," he said.

Freki had joined Haakon at the prow. Much as he still disliked his former 'accomplice', he couldn't help thinking that he looked pretty cool right now and tried to mirror his manly posture and determinedly jutting jawline.

He was interrupted in this somewhat comical endeavour by Haakon suddenly shouting, "Odd Sea ahoy!".

Indeed, the sea just ahead was turning rapidly pinker and coruscating in coral splendour in the sun, now fully risen.

As they advanced, the boat began to rock alarmingly and, as Torsten looked over the side, he could see vast, vague shapes looming ominously in the water and passing beneath the hull, causing the peculiar rocking motion.

"What is it, Uncle T?" asked BJ, frantically turning the wheel to compensate for a particularly nasty knock that sent the boat lurching perilously to starboard.

"Erm …," said Torsten, for want of something better or more nautical to say.

"Okay, Pen," said Freki, apparently unfazed by this turn of events, "do your stuff."

Penelope walked to the prow with surprising ease for a landlubber on a bucking bronco boat ride.

The others gazed at her, to the extent possible, whilst lurching inelegantly from side to side, with undisguised awe and Freki said, "You ain't seen nothing yet. This is gonna be really cool, man."

He and Haakon moved aside as Penelope reached the prow. She spread her arms wide and began to sing in a pure, lilting voice. The song was unlike anything her companions (besides Freki) had ever heard and was so heart-achingly beautiful that it brought tears to their many eyes.

After a few moments, the boat stopped its sickening lurch and the shadows in the rose-tinted water below dispersed. As the soul-searing song continued, they were replaced by something else: solid, black shapes were now swimming alongside the boat. Suddenly, they broke water, arching gracefully in the air and hitting the water again with an almighty splash that soaked the stunned sailors. They did this repeatedly, until finally, they all surfaced simultaneously, enabling the bedraggled crew of the Blomsthilda to get a better look at them.

Their bodies were stocky, sleek and dolphin-like, and their heads also, at first sight, if a little rounder in the snout. Penelope stopped singing and BJ took advantage of the silence and relative calm to leave the helm to take a closer look at the creatures, who were staying afloat with their upper bodies partially out of the water by rhythmically beating their tails backwards and forwards.

"Well, they seem friendly enough," he said. "Actually, they're quite cute."

As if by common accord, the creatures opened their mouths, or their heads, to be more precise. They opened outwards in four parts, like flower petals, to reveal a circle of terrifyingly sharp teeth. There was a collective intake of breath.

"Maybe not so cute after all," said BJ, hastening back to the helm.

The others had instinctively moved back towards the middle of the deck, except for Penelope and Freki, who were leaning over the railing petting the heads of the creatures, who had obligingly closed them and seemed to be enjoying the attention.

"Are you sure that's a good idea?" asked Torsten in an unnaturally squeaky voice.

Freki turned to him and grinned and Penelope said, "It alright now, Torsten, man. Dese be dolphinium. Dey da same creatures dat ma Tipp-Tippoldemor befriended and who helped her and her parents cross da Odd Sea safely all dem moon ago."

"Of course," said BJ, "you've already seen this happen, Frek, when you went with Penelope to try out the song."

"Yeah," said his friend, not taking his eyes off the curious creatures. "It's magic, man, and these guys are seriously cool."

He kissed Penelope appreciatively on the forehead.

"Da song work alright," she smiled. "Dey won' harm us now. In fact, dey swim wid us all da way to da islan' an' protect us."

The other dolphiniums all crowded round, wanting to be stroked too. They emitted a low sound, halfway between a bark and a grunt, and then splashed back into the water, soaking them all once more, before swimming rapidly ahead of the boat, jumping in and out of the water, stopping every now and then as if waiting for them to follow.

It was a beautiful day and the sun shone brightly, turning the sea around them an even deeper shade of pink. The winds were favourable and they were now making good headway.

A few hours passed uneventfully and then Haakon shouted, "Land ahoy!".

Ahead of them, they saw a narrow peninsula bounded by rocky outcrops. They heard the singing before they spied the sylph-like figures perched on the rocks. It was the same haunting melody that Penelope had sung to charm the dolphiniums, who had by this time turned and headed back into the deeper waters behind them.

As they sailed closer, they saw that the figures were women; the heads and torsos at least. In place of legs, however, they sported long tails made up of a myriad of multicoloured scales that shimmered in the sunlight reflected on the water beneath them. Their skin was translucent and the long, luscious locks flowing over their bare shoulders and breasts were the same vibrant pink colour as the ocean.

"Wow," breathed BJ and whistled appreciatively, eliciting a disapproving look from Penelope and a chuckle from Freki, which elicited another disapproving look, this time in his direction.

"Who are they? What are they?" asked Torsten, his eyes shining once more with tears at the beauty of the fish-tailed figures and their song.

"Dey is da Nereides," said Penelope. "Dey controls da sea and everytin' in it."

Oblivious to the danger, under the spell of the siren song, BJ was inadvertently steering the Blomsthilda dangerously close to the rocks. Penelope returned to the prow and began to sing in perfect unison with the lissom ladies on the lichen-covered rocks. They stopped as soon as they heard Penelope's sweet voice blending with their own, surprise registering in the green, glittering pools of their large, almond-shaped eyes.

Torsten had given the order to luff the sails to slow the boat down, but in spite of that, they were still drifting dangerously close to the rocks. Suddenly, however, at a gesture from one of the Nereides, the wind dropped completely and the Blomsthilda slowed to a halt. BJ awoke from his trance and hastily dropped the anchor to prevent them from drifting.

The Nereid who had stopped the wind appeared to be their leader. She was sitting higher than the others and was wearing a necklace of iridescent pearls and a crown of shells in her beautiful hair, whereas the others were unadorned. She slipped gracefully from her perch and dived into the sea in one swift, smooth motion, surfacing near the boat, her hair swirling like a seaweed fan in the water around her. Her voice, when she addressed them, was like a ripple of waves. She spoke in a strange language apparently unknown to them, but to the collective astonishment of all but Penelope, she answered, faltering slightly, but the Nereid seemed to understand her halting speech as she smiled and nodded.

"Err Pen," said Freki, who had watched this exchange with a look of rapt confusion on his yellowish-green face, "what's going on?"

Penelope took his hand and smiled reassuringly, saying, "It da lingo of me ancestors. Dey was forced to speak it as slaves on da islan'. My mamma speaks it an' even teaches it at da school. Dat's how ah knows it and it all comin' back to me now."

"And what did she say to you?" asked Haakon, still looking grim. "Does she know where Calypso is?"

"She jus' aksed me how ah knows da siren song, an' so ah tol' her. Dat all."

"Ask her about Calypso," barked Haakon. "I need to find her."

"And the others," Torsten reminded him.

Haakon nodded grimly in assent. Grimness seemed to have taken root in his psyche and was evidently germinating little baby grimness shoots, or "groots", Freki thought. He imagined little tendrils growing out of his ear and nose holes and twining around his head and neck.

He was roused from this strange but mildly amusing vision by Penelope speaking again to the Nereid queen, who responded, pointing towards the bay at the end of the peninsula and a narrow, pristine beach, the white sand glimmering in the sunlight. Then she turned and made a sign to her companions and, like a group of seriously stylish synchronised swimmers, they dived neatly, one after the other, surfacing briefly to smile and wave at the bemused onlookers, then plunging beneath the rippling waves, splashing their beautiful tails once before disappearing completely into the pinky depths.

"Well?" said Haakon impatiently as soon as they had gone.

"Dey on da islan' alright," Penelope replied. "Da Nereides 'as granted us permission to enter unharmed, but cannot guarantee our safety once we are dere."

Haakon clenched his fists and growled, "I cannot guarantee their safety once I get my hands on those drittbags."

He strode quickly to the cabin and came back wielding one of the bats he used to play nutball with his pupils.

"Let's go," he said.

Freki could almost see the tendrils tightening around the thick veins in his neck, distended with tension.

They rowed into the bay. As they approached the beach, it seemed deserted. The only sounds were the waves lapping against the shore and the distant call of a bird from somewhere in the trees lining the beach. As they rounded the final promontory, which had obscured their view of the bay in its entirety, they all gasped to see, rising majestically from the middle of the island, a massive, craggy mountain. The peak was so high it was lost in the clouds. Perched at an almost impossible angle on the side of the mountain was an imposing building, half palace, half castle, with ornate turrets and columns, dominated by a vast, domed tower and a wide, stone staircase built into the mountainside leading up to it. The whole edifice gleamed in the sunlight with a metallic glare, which made it impossible to look at for long.

"What the dritt?" said BJ, setting down his oars and rubbing his eyes.

"Limp Puss," said Penelope simply. "Bestemor tol' me 'bout dit place."

Freki suppressed a giggle when he saw the serious look on her face.

Finally, they reached the gravelly shore and pulled the rowing boat up onto the sand. As they looked around, they became aware that the beach was not deserted as they had previously thought. Standing quietly in the shadow of the treeline was an old man in a long, white robe.

CHAPTER TWO

The mystery of Mount Limp Puss

"Greetings, visitors!" said the man, his two eyes twinkling and his wrinkled face wrinkling even further in a welcoming smile.

The visitors gaped. He was evidently neither Traansylvanian nor Bestefarian, yet everyone understood what he said. He moved out of the shadows towards them and they could see that he had long, grey hair with a beard to match and appeared to be leaning on what looked to be some kind of staff.

"You speak our language," said Torsten, yellowish-green with wary curiosity.

"Indeed, indeed," boomed the man with a voice surprisingly sonorous for his apparently advanced age.

"I speak many languages, or rather, I speak and somehow it gets translated. Rather clever, really. But pray do tell, how came you here? We get so few visitors on the island."

"Not that surprising, really," said BJ, now considering that it was safe to speak, "given that you've effectively booby-trapped the ocean with ferocious beasties."

The old man was about to speak, but Haakon now approached him, gripping the nutball bat and banging it menacingly against the palm of his other hand.

"Where's Calypso?" he growled.

Freki made a mental note to practice that later, but in the meantime, he moved with the others to make sure Haakon didn't hurt the seemingly harmless old man.

"Calypso?" the old man repeated, shaking his head and looking a little dazed.

"The concealed one?"

"Aha!" said Haakon, taking a step closer. "Where have you concealed her? Tell me, old man, or I'll …"

As he spoke, he raised the nutball bat and the old man retaliated instinctively, raising the staff he had been holding, which suddenly emitted a crackle and a flash of light which lifted Haakon clean off his feet and threw him backwards into the sand.

"Sorry about that," said the old man. "Happens sometimes when I get stressed."

Torsten rushed to Haakon's side and was relieved to see that he was still breathing.

Seeing how pale he and his companions were, the old man sighed and said, "All is well. He's simply stunned. He'll be fine in a few moments."

And indeed, Haakon was already stirring, trying to lift his head, his hands searching ineffectually around him for his bat, which had been knocked several feet away. He slumped back onto the sand, groaning with pain and frustration.

"Forgive Me," said the old man. "It is incumbent upon Us to show hospitality to Our guests, no matter how rare or irate they may be. Perhaps you would care for some food and wine after your journey?"

He clapped his hands with the sound of a thunderbolt and suddenly, they found themselves in a large, luxurious banqueting hall before a vast, marble-topped table groaning with platters of meat, fruit and pitchers of wine. They all blinked, unbelieving, as Haakon was seated by two scantily-clad slaves in a high-backed wooden chair and propped up with velvet cushions.

"Xenia," the old man addressed one of the slave girls, "if you would do the honours."

The girl called Xenia clapped her hands and they winced, but all that happened was that more slaves appeared as if from nowhere with bowls of warm water for them to wash themselves.

"Dey all Bestafarian," whispered Penelope to Freki, "but ah don' reconise any of 'em."

Haakon was gazing blearily at Xenia.

"Calypso," he whispered hoarsely and tried to stand up.

Two heavily muscled male slaves on either side of him pushed him back down and he was too weak to resist.

"Please, My friends," said the old man, "eat, drink, enjoy."

He himself sat down at the other side of the table and handed his staff to one of the slaves, who promptly took it away.

"Uncle T," whispered BJ, "wasn't that a golf club?"

Torsten was about to reply, but Haakon began mumbling inarticulately again. The old man made a sign and Xenia took an exotic-looking fruit from beneath a covered platter and waved it enticingly in front of Haakon's nose holes. He sniffed the fruit and then, to everyone's surprise, began guzzling it with astonishing gusto. He then promptly fell asleep with his head lolling to one side, a beatific smile on his face and fruit juice dribbling down his pink chin.

"Do not be alarmed," said the old man, helping himself to a succulent bunch of grapes. "The food is not poisoned, but I would recommend steering clear of the lotus fruit. It does have some … interesting properties. When your friend awakes, he will feel much better … calmer, at least."

Torsten could bear it no longer.

"Where are we?" he said, the slightly squeaky tone back in his voice. "And who are you?"

"It is customary," said the old man, pouring himself a flagon of ruby-coloured wine, "to feast first and ask questions later."

Torsten decided that, for the moment, digestion was the better part of valour and, unable to resist the delicious-looking delicacies any longer, he gave the nod to the others and they fell on the food gratefully. The slaves served them wine, but they drank little, wanting to keep their wits about them for whatever was to come.

Once they had eaten their fill, the old man finally said, "Xenia, will you please go and fetch Hera."

To his guests (apart from Haakon, who was still sleeping soundly and snoring gently), he said, "I think My wife will be able to answer your questions better than I. I am old and, in spite of My illustrious parentage, get a little confused about the order of events."

A door opened at the other end of the banquet hall and in swept an elderly but still strikingly beautiful and surprisingly tall woman. Her long, black hair was streaked with grey and held back with a simple gold band. She wore a shorter version of the robe the old man was wearing and was carrying what appeared to be a tennis racquet.

"What is it, dear?" she said as she padded across the vast room in her simple but stylish leather sandals. "I was just about to have a quick game with Athena."

She stopped dead when she reached the table.

"Oh darling, why didn't You tell me We had guests? I look an absolute sight."

"You look beautiful as always, Hera," smiled the man.

The woman smiled back and sat next to her husband, placing her tennis racquet on the table in front of her.

Xenia came to pour her some wine, but she put her hand over the golden goblet and said, "Just water for Me."

She looked at her guests and patted her exquisitely flat tummy.

"I'm watching My weight."

She took a dainty sip of the water Xenia poured for her and there was a pause while she studied the multicoloured faces on the other side of the table and registered Haakon's slumbering state.

"Lotus fruit?" she asked her husband.

He nodded. She directed her gaze at Torsten, who was sitting directly opposite her.

"Are you from There?" she asked. "You're wearing those peculiar hats."

She puckered her already slightly puckered mouth with distaste.

"If you mean the Otherland," said Torsten, "then sort of. We're looking for some friends of ours who were... erm ...."

"Stolen," said Penelope with unusual force. "You people always stealin' people from our islan' and usin' dem as slaves. It outrageous, man!"

Freki nodded and took her hand. The old man looked slightly uncomfortable.

He turned to his wife and said, "I thought We'd stopped doing that, dearest."

His wife shrugged haughtily.

"We needed some new blood, darling," she said "Can't have them all interbreeding now, can We?"

"So you are the Theoi?" said BJ, his four eyes wide with shock. "You don't look very powerful to me."

Torsten gave him a warning look, remembering the earlier electrifying incident on the beach, but the woman just smiled enigmatically.

The old man shuffled in his seat and said, "I believe We are being remiss once again. Xenia, coffee, please."

Once coffee was served, hot and strong enough to stand a spoon in, the old man said, "And now perhaps it is time for some introductions."

He looked expectantly at Torsten, who cleared his throat and introduced himself and his entourage as it were any normal social occasion. He was about to continue when Haakon suddenly awoke with a start and looked around with a dazed expression on his face, which was the same yellowish hue as the fruit which was promptly put in his hand by a slave standing watchfully near his chair, and which was devoured with the same relish as the first. Haakon's eyes turned glassy and within minutes, his head was lolling against the back of the chair and he was sound asleep once more.

"What the dritt is that stuff?" asked BJ, mentally calculating how much he could make from selling it back home.

"Lotus fruit," replied Hera. "It's a natural tranquilliser. He'll be out of it for a while."

She shot a questioning look at her husband.

"He was waving that thing at Me," said the old man defensively, pointing to the nutball bat which had been brought in by one of the slaves, who was holding it deftly and looking like he wouldn't be afraid to use it if necessary.

"He was jus' tryin' to fin' his girlfrien', Calypso," said Penelope. "She one o' da girl dat ya took."

"Which brings us to why we are here," said Torsten. "Look, we don't want any trouble. We just want to take Calypso and the others back to where we came from."

"But Our slaves are very well treated," said Hera. "You're welcome to join them if you wish. You look healthy enough, strong and feisty. Especially him," she said with a flirtatious glance at Haakon.

Penelope's face was getting redder and redder and Torsten decided to try another tack.

"Perhaps you'd like to tell us about yourselves?" he said with what he hoped was a winning smile.

It was the right thing to do. The old man suddenly sat upright and looked taller, more imposing somehow. He spoke and his words resonated around the vast hall. Unfortunately, nobody could understand what he was saying, apart from Penelope, who looked slightly shell-shocked.

"Apologies," mumbled the man. "Our language always prevails when making important announcements. Let Me try again."

This time he stood up, made a sign in the air with his right hand and intoned, "I am Zeus, king of the Gods of Mount Olympus, and this is my wife and queen, Hera."

She nodded graciously in acknowledgement.

Freki nudged BJ and whispered, "Not Limp Puss, then."

He seemed disappointed.

"Gods?" squeaked Torsten.

He thought back to Baldursson, who hadn't really been a God at all but decided reasonably that, given the evidence, this was a totally feasible proposition. He was struck with a sudden thought. He drew himself up to his full height.

"I myself am considered a God in the Otherland," he declared, not entirely untruthfully.

The others, including Zeus, looked at him with surprise and Hera with undisguised incredulity.

"Yes," he continued, more confidently now. "They call me Bestefar."

One of the slaves gave a start, looked at Torsten and automatically gave the response, "Ya, man."

She was silenced by a withering look from Hera.

"See," said Torsten. "They remember."

He did his jazz hands thing. BJ nudged Freki, who nudged Penelope, and they all did it as if this were the most natural thing in the world.

Zeus was looking at Torsten with interest.

"And do you have any powers?" he asked.

Torsten was pleased to see that even Hera was looking a little rattled at this point.

"Well, I arrived on the Otherland from my .. err .. palace in Traansylvania in a flash of lightning," he said, hoping that sounded impressive enough.

"Well, bless Me!" said Zeus, sitting back down. "I am the God of Lightning," he said. "Among other things. At least …," he paused, "… I think I am."

He looked at Hera, who nodded, slightly sadly, Torsten thought. That would explain how he floored Haakon on the beach, he also thought.

Hera sighed.

"Maybe you could be of some use to Us," she said.

Zeus gave her what can only be described as a meaningful look.

She sighed again and said, more softly this time, "Maybe you could help Us."

There was a collective raising of eyebrows. Zeus took a noisy slurp of coffee and Hera began fiddling with the strings on her tennis racquet.

"Go to Athena and tell her We won't be playing today," she said to a slave boy hovering nearby.

He left the room and she sat further forward in her chair, running her ring-bedecked fingers distractedly through her hair.

"We also came from somewhere else," she began. "We are the Theoi, descended from a race of powerful, primordial deities called Titans. We took up residence on Mount Olympus. There was a great and terrible war for supremacy between Us and the Titans that lasted for ten long years. During the final battle, My husband got a bit carried away (Zeus looked a little sheepish at this point). He summoned a mighty storm, hoping to smite the enemy once and for all. I just remember seeing a tremendous bolt of lightning heading towards Us and the next thing I knew, We were here, on this island; still on Mount Olympus, but no longer in Our native land. It took Us a while to realise We had been transported. And not a Titan in sight."

She paused then, tears sparkling in her beautiful brown eyes. Torsten actually started feeling a bit sorry for her.

"We used to have such power," she continued. "The humans were perfect pawns for Us in our games. We had such fun playing with them, messing with their plans, pitting them one against the other, placing bets between Us to see who would prevail."

She had a faraway look in her eyes now and Torsten suddenly stopped feeling sorry for her, his mind getting to grips instead with what she had just said.

"Humans?" he shouted, causing Haakon to stir briefly from his sleep and mutter something unintelligible. "You were on Earth?"

Penelope looked confused, but Hera suddenly felt several pairs of eyes boring into her, wide with surprise and delight.

"You know Earth?" Hera said.

Torsten nodded. "We have, sorry, *had* friends there," he replied.

Freki turned to Penelope and said, "It's a long story."

As Torsten didn't seem willing to expand on this, Hera continued, "We discovered that Our powers are severely diminished here for some reason. Also, time moves slowly in this place, but it does move, and We are, alas, no longer immortal. Food and fresh water We have in abundance, but no Ambrosia, which bestows longevity on you mortals and immortality upon Us. Our slaves were gradually dying and We had to find a solution, so We sent the last of them out on scouting missions to see what was across the seas. Three parties came back with nothing to report and one came back with sightings of an island to the east of Us peopled with, well, you, and that's when We put together Our plan.

We only stole a few of you at a time; young, strong and preferably vaguely aesthetically pleasing (she cast her eye briefly over Haakon's sleeping form once again). To make sure you didn't come looking for them, We used what remains of Our powers to make the ocean that separates Us as daunting and difficult to cross as possible. Fortunately, the Nereides were transported with Us and are a great help with security, and We did have some fun fabricating the fascinating and fearsome flora and fauna, which you somehow seem to have avoided to get here, not to mention Our lovely ladies with their lethal lullabies. You must tell Me how you did that, by the way, so that We can stop it from happening again."

Hera seemed to have run out of steam by this time and her audience was silent, trying to take it all in.

Zeus, who had been nodding along as his wife told the story, finally broke the silence.

"I am old," he said, "and My powers are weak and unpredictable."

He gestured towards Haakon at this point, who was drooling.

"Long have I tried to reproduce the conditions which brought Us here to take Us back to Earth, but in vain."

He turned to Torsten.

"Can you help Us?" he asked, hope shining in his slightly cloudy eyes.

Torsten knew as well as his companions that there was nothing they could do, no matter how much they longed to see their human friends again. However, he also knew that if he admitted this, they would lose any bargaining power they may have over their hosts.

And so, after a suitable pause, he said, "This requires some serious discussion between my … acolytes and myself."

BJ balked a little at this, but Penelope, understanding what Torsten was up to, put a warning hand on his arm.

"We need to know firs' of all dat our friends are safe," she said.

The others nodded approvingly.

"Very well," said Hera after a brief whispered conversation with her husband.

"We will take you to them. But the hour grows late, and I think we would all benefit from a good night's sleep after the day's excitement. Our finest rooms are at your disposal and tomorrow, We will give you a proper tour of the island. You can meet the family and see for yourselves that your people are perfectly alright. Is that agreeable to everyone?"

Torsten spoke for everyone when he replied that her suggestion was perfectly acceptable.

"What about Sleeping Beauty?" said BJ, jerking his head in Haakon's direction.

"Fear not, he will be taken care of," said Zeus, rising laboriously from his chair.

"More fruit?" asked Freki with a grin.

Zeus nodded and his face crinkled in a smile. He and Hera quite cordially wished them a good night and they were shown to their sumptuous sleeping quarters. Torsten fell gratefully into the first comfortable bed he had slept in for as long as he could remember, but in spite of his exhaustion, sleep eluded him for some time. It might have been partly the fault of the coffee, which he was unused to drinking, but mostly, his mind was churning over the events of the day and he was still trying to think of a plan to get them all safely out of this somewhat surreal situation when he finally fell into a deep and dreamless sleep.

CHAPTER THREE

Homer's Beach

"Good morning," said Hera breezily as she swept onto the beautiful, colonnaded terrace where her guests were tucking into a most excellent and bountiful breakfast.

They mumbled their greetings through mouthfuls of the delicious food.

"Please excuse My husband's absence," she said. "He was rather perturbed by yesterday's events and went out for an early round of golf."

"I told you it was a golf club," whispered BJ to Torsten.

"You have a golf course?" said Freki, helping himself to another fresh bread roll.

"But of course," answered Hera, holding out her cup for Xenia to pour the coffee. "No pun intended."

She laughed a pleasant, tinkling laugh. "It's down by Homer's Beach."

"Cool," said Freki.

Penelope had eaten little and was anxious to get going.

"How Haakon doin'?" she asked Hera.

The others started guiltily. Torsten realised with a pang of remorse that he hadn't given the poor chap a thought since he'd awoken feeling refreshed and ravenously hungry.

"If you mean the handsome one, he's still sleeping," replied Hera. "I was told that he got rather … restless during the night and was required to partake of …."

"Another fruit fix?" suggested Freki.

Hera bowed her head in assent.

"Cool," said Freki.

"Den we bring Calypso to him an' 'e be feelin' betta," said Penelope decisively.

"Very well," said Hera, "I suggest you hold on to those hideous hats of yours."

She clapped her hands and with the sound of a thunderbolt, they found themselves standing next to a tennis court where a noisy game seemed to be in progress. They were in bright sunlight, but when they shaded their eyes and looked up, they could see the towers of the palace glittering high above them. They looked back at Hera, blinking with surprise and temporary sun blindness.

She shrugged nonchalantly.

"Just a small trick I picked up from My husband," she said.

When their vision had cleared, they took a closer look at the pair battling it out on the tennis court. An extremely handsome and well-built male with short, blond curls, shiny with sweat, was berating himself for having just smashed a shot over the line, losing him the game. The female, whose hair was darker and longer but equally curly, tumbling from beneath a somewhat outlandish metal helmet, was laughing and they distinctly heard her tell her partner that that was not a wise choice of shot. He promptly threw his racquet on the ground in a rage and broke it, which just made him even angrier, launching a volley of unintelligible verbal vitriol, which made Penelope blush pinky-purple.

"May I present Ares and Athena," said Hera. "Half-siblings. Their exchanges are always spirited."

They left the courts and the cursing behind them and walked down a tree-lined path which led to a flat, open, green area where another stunning couple were busy shooting arrows at a series of targets a fair distance away from them. The arrows were hurtling towards the targets with incredible speed and precision. They looked strikingly similar, with the same chiselled features and long, wavy hair, except that hers was slightly darker and held back with the same type of gold band that Hera was wearing.

"Apollo and Artemis," said Hera. "They're twins."

She moved on and the others followed. Every now and then, a slave would hurry past carrying baskets of food or large pots and jugs, pausing only to bow to Hera. Penelope looked at each of them eagerly but then shook her head and continued walking. One slave was even holding a small, woolly, black creature which was struggling in his arms and bleating plaintively. Penelope gasped.

"Isn't that an ullabeist?" said Torsten.

"Ya, man," said Penelope.

She turned to Hera.

"Ah s'pose you stole dem from us too."

Hera considered this for a moment.

"Hmm … yes, well, We only took a few, for breeding, you understand. They're rather tasty, as you know, because you had them for dinner last night."

Nobody could really object to this because the Bestefarians also bred the ullabeistene for their meat, as well as their wool.

Hera then led them off the path through a gateway half-hidden by foliage. It reminded Torsten painfully of the secret garden in Misselthwaite, back on Earth. It was a beautiful, big garden, filled with olive trees and vines and colourful, exotic plants, which happily didn't remind Torsten painfully of the secret garden in Misselthwaite. In the midst of this lush, luxuriant splendour stood a tall, willowy woman in a green robe with long, flowing hair the colour of ripened wheat in the sunshine, slightly streaked with grey and adorned with a garland of fresh flowers. Her skin was deeply bronzed and had that crepey texture which comes from spending too much time in the sun. She was cutting heavy bunches of huge, succulent grapes from the vines and handing them to a slave who was heaping them into a basket. She smiled at Hera and waved.

"That's Demeter," said Hera, not returning the wave. "She likes gardening."

They would have liked to stay a while in the pleasant, shady garden, but Hera seemed to be in a hurry to leave, so they followed her down another winding path towards a long, low, stone building with clouds of smoke belching from a large chimney in the centre of the roof.

Torsten wondered vaguely if this was where the slaves were quartered, but Hera rapidly put an end to this chain of thought by announcing, "This is the Forge of Hephaestus."

They entered and were instantly struck by a wave of heat emanating from the enormous firepit, which was tended by an elderly but still attractive, buxom woman with a shock of red hair that seemed to dance around her beautiful face along with the flames. Next to her stood a powerful, bare-chested man, the dark curls in his hair and beard damp with sweat, banging with fierce intensity on a piece of metal at the anvil. He held it up and scrutinised it for a moment and they could see that it was a beautifully crafted golf driver before he resumed his vigorous hammering. They were so focused on their forging that they didn't even notice they were being observed.

"Hestia and Hephaestus," said Hera "He used to make our weapons, but We don't need those any more, so now He just makes whatever We want."

She pointed to the neat rows of sports equipment behind him, together with piles of pots, plates, kitchen utensils and other miscellaneous metal items.

"He's awfully good with wood too," she added. "And Hestia just likes being by the fire."

They were all relieved to be out of the searing heat of the forge. Torsten noticed that Hera hadn't even broken a sweat whilst his robe was dripping and his face burning. He felt like he'd been boiled and the others didn't look much better. They had very quickly removed their warm, woolly Bestefarian hats and poor Penelope was fanning herself ineffectually with hers.

"You look like a bunch of over-ripe tomatoes," said Hera, laughing her tinkly laugh.

Seeing their damp displeasure, however, she suggested they go to the pool to freshen up, to which they all eagerly agreed. A mercifully shady path led down from the forge to a beautiful, natural basin at the foot of a tall cliff from which cascaded a stream of fresh water. It looked deliciously cool and inviting.

"This is Aphrodite's Pond," said Hera. "And yes, you may bathe," she said, responding to a beseeching look from BJ.

He and Freki whooped and jumped straight in, closely followed by the others, though Hera stayed on the side and watched them splashing about with detached amusement. As BJ struck out towards the far end of the pond, he swallowed a mouthful of water in surprise when he saw a girl sitting on a rock, combing her long, golden hair. She was the most beautiful creature BJ had ever seen, and she was stark naked.

He coughed and she looked at him with her huge, slightly slanting eyes, as bright and blue as the cloudless sky above them. Time seemed to stand still and BJ trod water, taking in the breathtaking sight before him; the maiden's alabaster skin, her perfect curves, her cute upturned nose, her rosebud mouth. The bubble only burst when he heard Freki calling his name. He sighed and turned to swim back to where the others were standing at the side of the pond, wringing out their wet garments. As BJ clambered out, soggy and starstruck, he caught Hera's eye and she gave him a knowing smile.

Penelope was getting impatient.

"Can we see da oders now? Ya promised," she said to Hera.

"Patience, Penelope," replied Hera. "We are almost there."

She pointed to a path a little way beyond the pond.

"Just down there is Homer's Beach. The slave huts are right next to it. As I told you, they are very well treated and their accommodation perfectly comfortable."

"Yeah, but they're still slaves," said Freki.

He looked round at BJ for support, but he didn't answer and seemed lost in thought.

"Ya, man," said Penelope, taking Freki's arm.

Hera shrugged and walked on ahead, nimbly negotiating the rocky path which was winding down towards the sea. They could now hear the sound of breaking waves, and before long, the path ended, and they found themselves standing on a white, sandy shore with the pink sea shimmering before them.

Sitting on a deckchair in the middle of the beach was a fat, bearded man with ruddy cheeks and a mop of dark curls topped with a winged helmet. He was gazing out to sea and sipping from a large, golden cup.

"Hello there," he hiccuped jovially when he caught sight of Hera and her colourful companions.

"Would you care for a cup of wine? It's awfully good. Dionysus has excelled himself this time."

As if to prove his point, he took a good slug, wiped his beard and waved his cup at them invitingly.

"No, thank you, dear," said Hera, "And it looks like You've had quite enough already."

The fat man chuckled and addressed the others.

"Are you here for the game?" he asked. "It's about to start, and I think it's going to be epic."

They looked nonplussed, and Hera replied, "How appropriate, given the location, but actually, We're just passing through."

Suddenly, there was the sound of a horn being blown. An enormous man with curly, jet-black hair and a beard to match, rippling with muscles, had surfaced out of nowhere from the sea in front of them. In one hand, he was holding a long, lethal-looking trident and in the other was a giant conch shell, which he was blowing into to make the horn sound. Around him appeared the Nereides, who waved at the group of gawping spectators, and the dolphiniums, who splashed in and out of the water, somersaulting, flapping their fins and grunt-barking their greetings.

When the man spoke, it was like the crashing of waves against the rocks.

"Right," he boomed, "I want a good, fair game. No cheating like last time, alright?"

He was looking directly at the Nereides queen as he said this, and she pouted and tossed her beautiful hair. The giant then waved his trident, and the conch disappeared to be replaced with a massive sea urchin shell, which he then tossed into the water.

One of the dolphiniums got to it first and batted it with its snout towards another, but before it got there, it was intercepted by a Nereid, who tapped it neatly to one of her team-mates. Back and forth sailed the ball, followed carefully by the big man who was riding on the back of what can only be described as a giant eel, hanging on one-handed to a pair of seaweed reins, waving his trident and blowing every now and then on the conch shell, which had reappeared, to indicate a foul.

One of the dolphiniums finally leapt spectacularly out of the water and caught the ball with a cracking blow of its tail, sending it spinning off and landing neatly between two gigantic wooden posts which had risen unobtrusively out of the water, eliciting a cacophony of grunting barks from one team and high-pitched squeals of frustration from the other.

"Goal," screamed the fat man, leaping from his deck chair and spilling wine all over his already non too clean robe in the process.

Hera sighed and turned away, signalling the others to follow, although they were actually quite enjoying the match.

As they left, she said, "I do love Poseidon, but I absolutely loath sea polo."

"Who was the fat dude in the chair?" asked Freki as they walked.

"Oh, that was Hermes," said Hera "He used to be our messenger, but now He can't go anywhere, so He just sits around eating and drinking and watching sport. Sad, really."

"I really dug his helmet," said Freki.

Hera looked confused, but they had now reached a series of wooden huts with brightly painted shutters and covered porches at the front, complete with swing chairs.

"Your friends are in the training hut at the moment with Hebe," said Hera. "She's our head cupbearer and also responsible for training the new slaves."

They entered one of the bigger huts towards the rear of the complex. It reminded them all of the little village school back in the Otherland. Inside the surprisingly large, light room, a small group of Bestefarians was sitting on wooden benches, attentively listening to a beautiful young woman with sandy-coloured hair pulled back into an elaborate bun, saying a series of phrases, which the Bestefarians obediently repeated.

"Language class," whispered Hera.

At this, the young woman looked up and smiled. The Bestefarians turned, and their faces all went as pink as the ocean outside with pleasure when they saw who was there. One of the trainee slave girls ran towards Penelope and hugged her.

"Where Haakon?" she said, a yellow tinge of worry creeping across her complexion. "Did 'e not come wid ya?"

"Calypso, tank Bestefar y'alright," said Penelope. "Don' worry, Haakon is 'ere, but 'e got into a spot o' trouble an' is back at da palace under guard."

"Ahem," said the young teacher, coming towards them, looking cross at the disruption to her class.

"It's alright, Hebe," said Hera imperiously. "I told them they could come and make sure their friends are safe and sound. You may leave Us."

Hebe bowed to Hera and left the room.

"So, are you satisfied?" asked Hera.

Penelope nodded but said, "For now. But Haakon mus' see Calypso. Oderwise 'e be eatin' dat fruit and sleepin' for da res' of 'is life."

Calypso looked at her enquiringly, but Hera said, "We will wake him when We get back to the palace, and then you can reassure your cute but comatose companion that We will all be together this evening. My husband has a little surprise for you."

"Did she say 'cute'," whispered Calypso to Penelope.

"Ya, man, but don' worry," Penelope whispered back. "He only 'ave eyes for you, Calpyso. He wouldn' rest until we came to find ya."

Calypso smiled, and Hera said, "Right, that's all settled then. We'll leave your little friends to continue their training. Don't worry, you will see them later. As I said, Zeus has prepared a surprise for this evening, and you'll be wanting to freshen up and have a bite to eat. We'll pick Him up on the way."

With that, she swept out of the room and nodded to Hebe, who was waiting outside. The others left reluctantly and followed Hera across a pleasant park behind the huts. As they reached a row of very tall trees at the end of the park, they distinctly heard someone shout, "Fore", and a moment later, a golf ball clipped the trunk of the tree directly ahead of them and bounced off into the undergrowth.

"Nice shot, dear," said Hera as Zeus appeared, looking flustered and rummaging through the bushes with his golf club.

"Hmph," said Zeus, "that's the seventh one I've lost today."

"Let's go home, dear, and have a rest and a small feast, and then You can tell Our guests all about Your surprise," said Hera.

"Surprise?" he said, handing his club to a slave caddy standing nearby. "Oh yes, the surprise."

His cloudy old eyes suddenly lit up with delight, and he clapped his hands. With the sound of a thunderbolt, they found themselves back in the banqueting hall.

"I will never get used to that," moaned Torsten.

CHAPTER FOUR

Rhapsody in Pink

"We're having a beach party," declared Zeus, happily gnawing at a massive meat bone, which he then threw in the direction of a monstrous three-headed dog who was dozing by the huge, empty hearth.

One of the heads caught it neatly, and the other two glared at it balefully.

"Cool," said Freki.

"To what do we owe the honour?" asked Torsten.

He was feeling a little anxious as he hadn't yet worked out any plan of escape or what he was going to say to their hosts if they asked for help again.

"A celebration," said Hera, "to welcome you to Mount Olympus. Nothing more."

Torsten strongly suspected that there was a hidden agenda but decided to just go with the flow for now. He had checked BJ's mobile phone the previous evening, but they were way too far away from Traansylvania to get a signal, so no chance of getting a message to Dordi. He thought wistfully about Hermes' winged helmet but had understood from Hera that it was useless here.

Haakon had finally been woken by being dunked unceremoniously in a bath of cold water and was now recovering in his room, watched over by two strapping slaves, just in case. He felt sick and hungover, but was calm now and relieved to hear from Penelope that Calypso was well and that he would see her that evening. Hera had confirmed that the recently abducted Bestefarians would be graciously given an evening off from training to join them at the party.

They all had a nap after the midday meal, apart from Haakon, who was tired of sleeping, and then they bathed and put on the fresh, clean robes that had been left on their beds. Torsten had requested an emergency meeting in his room prior to the party. Haakon couldn't come, of course, as he was still heavily guarded, but everyone else duly gathered in Torsten's room in all their finery.

"What's up, Uncle T?" said BJ. "Have you thought of a plan?"

"Sadly not," said Torsten. "I was hoping that you bright, young things might have come up with some ideas, especially you, BJ, with your talent for gaming strategy."

BJ didn't know what to say. He hadn't told anyone, even Freki, about the divine (literally, in this case) apparition at the pond, but he hadn't been able to think about anything else since. Penelope and Freki looked at each other and shrugged ruefully.

Torsten sighed.

"I'll think of something. In the meantime, keep your wits about you at the party tonight. And keep playing the Bestefar card. It's the only thing we've got at the moment."

"Ya, man," said Penelope.

"Good girl," smiled Torsten and did his jazz hands thing.

They walked down the imposing marble staircase to find Zeus, Hera and Haakon, pink-faced, fresh and smart in a clean, white robe, waiting for them.

"Ready?" said Zeus, and they closed their eyes, waiting for the inevitable.

One clap of thunder later, they were back on the beach where they had been earlier that day. It looked quite different now, with the sun going down in a blaze of glory, turning the sea a deep, reddish pink. Fires were burning merrily here and there, and there was a delightful smell of roasting meat and the sound of cheerful chatter.

Calypso spotted Haakon straight away and ran into his arms. Hera motioned for two guards to watch them, and the rest of them walked along the beach to find the group of Gods and Goddesses they had glimpsed briefly that morning, all standing or sitting around a long table surrounded by flaming torches, looking gorgeous, drinking wine and discussing the games they were going to play the next day. They stopped when they saw Zeus and Hera approaching and stared with unabashed curiosity at their guests. Hera made the introductions but refrained from telling them why they had come to the island.

Drinks were brought, and there was a brief, uncomfortable silence. Then Hermes wove his way up to them in a clean, white robe, evidently already a little the worse for wear, arm in arm with another chubby, cheeky-looking chap similar in looks to himself but for the crown of vine leaves twined around his dark, curly hair.

He grabbed a golden cup from a tray held by a slave and, after taking a deep swig of the contents, said, "I don't believe you've met Dionysus, My half-brother. He's the God of wine, so very handy to have around, and the master maker of that divine brew that you are currently sampling. Isn't that right, Di?"

He followed this with a quite spectacular belch.

Dionysus chuckled and greeted them jovially.

"So what brings you to Our island, friends?" he asked, prompting a sharp intake of breath from Hera. "And how in Hades did you get past the perils and pitfalls We placed in the Pink Sea?"

"We can thank Pen for that," said Freki proudly. "She knows the siren song."

Hera scoffed.

"How can she possibly know the siren song?"

"Oh, Mother," said Ares disdainfully, "how else would they have got here, for Our sake?"

Penelope looked at Torsten in some consternation, but he nodded.

"Ma Great-Great-Great-Gran'moder escape from dis islan' wid her parent many, many moon ago. Dey was slaves here. She made friend wid da Nereides and dey taught her da song dat tame da creatures in da Odd Sea."

She got a blank look from the Theoi at this point, so she explained, "Dat wat we call your pink sea back home."

"Incredible," breathed Zeus.

He looked pleased, and the other Theoi looked impressed. Torsten was also pleased that nobody had mentioned his God-like status on the Otherland. He didn't wish to draw attention to it at this point in the proceedings.

Hebe then approached the group, looking a lot less schoolmarmish than she had earlier. Her hair was down now and tumbling in amber curls over one bare, bronzed shoulder, shown off to perfection by the asymmetrical white robe she was wearing.

"Dinner is served," she said. "If You would care to be seated, I will bring wine."

Hermes clapped his hands together happily. Everyone winced again, but nothing untoward happened.

"Where's that pretty Xenia?" he asked. "Got the night off?"

"Oh Hermes," said Hera, "You know Hebe is Our cupbearer on special occasions."

Hebe bowed and smiled graciously, but Torsten got the impression that she wasn't that thrilled about it.

Everyone was served more wine and some of the succulent, roasted meat, apart from Poseidon, who helped himself to a massive, whole fish. A pink-faced Haakon was brought to the table by his guards with an equally rosy-cheeked Calypso in tow and was introduced to the party by Hera.

"Ah, lotus-fruit man," said Ares and giggled.

Haakon went red, but Calypso put a steadying hand on his arm, and he just grunted.

"I see that Xenia is not the only one who has the night off, Mother," said Athena, rolling her eyes meaningfully towards Calypso.

"She is only a trainee, dear," replied Hera. "And I think Haakon here would be most put out if she weren't invited to join Us."

Athena arched her already perfectly arched eyebrows even further.

"This is why you came here, isn't it?" She addressed this last question to Torsten, who nodded.

Haakon was about to speak, but Torsten shot him a warning look, and he thought better of it. He wasn't eating much and kept sniffing his food suspiciously when he wasn't gazing adoringly at Calypso.

"You do know that slavery is bad, don't you?" said BJ through a mouthful of meat. Torsten groaned inwardly.

Hera bristled.

"Let me understand this correctly," she said. "I have been given to believe that all the slaves We have taken were servants on your island. Is that not so?"

Penelope nodded, and BJ said, "Yes, but being a servant and being a slave are very different things."

"How so?" said Hera.

"Well, slaves are unpaid labour," said BJ.

"And how do you pay your servants?" asked Hera. "Do you have coin on your island?"

"No, but they have free food and lodging," said BJ.

"So they are well treated," said Hera with the ghost of a smile. "But still servants. How does that make them any different from Our slaves?"

"Dey not stolen, for a start," Penelope intervened. "An' dey free to come and go as dey please. No-one make 'em be servants. It a matter o' choice, man."

It was Hera's turn to arch her eyebrows. She and her husband exchanged a glance, and there was another brief, uncomfortable silence, which was only broken by a belch from Hermes.

"Do any of you play tennis?" asked Ares suddenly.

Torsten was quite relieved at the somewhat surprising change of subject but was forced to say no; he'd never played in his life.

The others also shook their heads, apart from Haakon, who said, "I play a bit, but we're not planning to hang around here, are we?"

He looked at Torsten as he said this.

"I don't know," said Torsten uncertainly.

He exchanged a look with Hera, who said, "You may stay for as long as you wish."

"Splendid," said Ares. "I'm so bored with playing with this lot. They're all rubbish."

Athena snorted, and everyone laughed.

"So let me get this straight," said BJ. "All you do around here is play games and eat."

He indicated the copious amount of food on the table in front of him.

"And drink," said Hermes, raising his cup.

"There's not a lot to do, really," said Zeus, "since We lost most of Our powers and with no humans to play with ..."

He trailed off, stabbed moodily at an olive on his plate and missed.

"We do have some super games, though," piped up Apollo, speaking for the first time.

"Yes," agreed Artemis. "Jolly good fun. Maybe you'd like to join Us tomorrow."

"Cool," said Freki.

The rest of the dinner passed pleasantly enough, with no more touchy subjects being touched on. Afterwards, Freki, Penelope, Haakon and Calypso went for a paddle and splashed about happily in the surf. Torsten was sitting next to Zeus and was mulling over something that had been milling about in the back of his mind for a while. Something to do with Archibald Craven's magnificent, oak-panelled library with its floor-to-ceiling shelves crammed with all manner of books; a veritable haven of tranquillity with its deep, comfy armchairs arranged around the fireplace, the lingering perfume of pipe smoke and old paper.

"Why is this called Homer's Beach?" he asked.

"I can show you if you like," said Zeus, pushing himself up slowly from his chair and rubbing his back.

"Won't be long, dear," he said to Hera. "Little walk after dinner."

Hera nodded briefly and went back to her conversation with Hephaestus about tightening the tension on her tennis racquet.

Zeus and Torsten walked in companionable silence along the beach, preceded by a slave bearing a torch. They reached the foot of a cliff, and Zeus asked the slave to hold the torch up high to allow Torsten to see the monument before them. It was a large stone slab dominated by a statue of a robed man whose long beard made up for his lack of hair. On the tombstone, Torsten could just make out some symbols which he couldn't understand.

It reads, "Homer. His words will never die," said Zeus.

The library swam back into Torsten's mind; an old, leather-bound book in the history section, the name of which escaped him and which he had meant to read but never got around to.

"Homer," repeated Torsten.

"Yes, he was human," replied Zeus. "A bard; wonderful, clever man. Composed beautiful poetry and used to bring it up to Us on Olympus when he was but a young thing. We allowed him access when We realised how talented he was. He was transported here with Us but sadly struck blind by My lightning bolt, the poor chap. We asked him to live with Us, but he refused. He was a man of simple, almost ascetic tastes and preferred to live in a cave at the bottom of the mountain. We made sure that he was looked after, though, and he lived to a ripe old age actually, just there (he pointed to an opening in the cliff a little way above them). That's why we buried him here. Named the beach after him. Least we could do."

Zeus bowed his head in remembrance, and Torsten did the same, unsure what to say. Then, they heard the conch shell being blown from the beach behind them.

"They're calling Us back," said Zeus. "Appropriately enough, I think the entertainment is about to begin."

Torsten's curiosity was piqued. He hadn't been expecting entertainment at the party. He wondered if it was going to be another game, but it seemed a little dark now, even though the two moons were now high in the night sky.

They joined the others, who were all now seated looking out to sea. Torsten resigned himself to sitting through another polo match and so was totally unprepared for what came next.

The sea around the rocks a little way out from the beach began to glow, lighting up the Nereides who had been sitting unseen upon them. They began to sing, not the siren song this time, but a rhapsody about a long war amongst men and one brave warrior who spent ten years trying to get home to his devoted wife across the sea, battling against the odds, terrifying creatures and the whims of the Gods. Unfortunately, only Penelope could understand what they were singing about.

In spite of this, the audience barely noticed the time passing; it was so hauntingly beautiful.

At the end, they stood up and applauded, and the Nereides bowed and then dived gracefully back into the still-glowing waters.

"Wow," said Torsten, his cheeks wet with tears.

He couldn't help but think of Kim and how much he would have loved it.

"Well done, Di," said Hermes, clapping his half-brother heartily on the back.

"Yes, well done, old chap," echoed Zeus from his throne, which remarkably didn't look at all out of place on the beach. "Top hole!"

"You did this?" said Torsten, turning to Dionysus, who shrugged and said, "Can't take the credit for the writing – that was Our old friend, Homer - nor for the singing, of course, but the staging, yup, that was Me. Particularly proud of the luminous jellyfish lighting. I got Poseidon there to bring them up from the deep especially."

He raised his cup to toast his own success and downed the contents in one.

Torsten still looked confused, so Hermes put one hand heavily on his shoulder and slurred, "My half-brother isn't just a pretty face, you know (a chuckle from Dionysus at this). He's not only the God of wine but also the God of theatre!"

Torsten couldn't believe it. Theatre was his thing, and he resolved to have a chat with Dionysus about it at the earliest possible opportunity.

"It was pretty cool," said Freki. "But I didn't understand a dritting word of it."

Penelope gave them a summary, and Torsten, still with the mysterious book in his head, asked Zeus if it existed in written form.

"I'm afraid not, old chap," said Zeus. "Homer was a typical bard of the oral tradition. Their poems, stories and songs were passed down from generation to generation by word of mouth. Homer taught them to the Nereides, and who knows, maybe they will teach it to young Penelope here."

She smiled and nodded.

"Ah would love to write 'em down," she said. "Mebbe ya could help me now, Torsten man."

Torsten was thrilled. This was something he could do that Kim would be proud of; something to work on when he got home. If he ever got home, he thought, remembering the brave warrior in the song. He was so lost in thought that he wasn't even aware that Hera was standing next to him.

"So, Bestefar," she said quietly, "have you and your friends had time to think?"

This was the question that Torsten had been dreading. He looked at her, trying to ignore the hope that was shining in her beautiful eyes in the torchlight. He noticed that she was wearing an ornate, metal bracelet cleverly crafted in the shape of a snake. In the place of its head was an unusual blue stone. He remembered that Haakon still had the bracelet Petra had used to send him to the Otherland, and that gave him an idea.

"There is one possibility," he said carefully. "But it involves me and my friends getting home."

"To the Otherland," said Hera.

"I am not from the Otherland," said Torsten. "There is a land even beyond over the sea, and that is where BJ, Freki, Haakon and myself come from. There is someone there who might be able to help."

"We could go with you," said Hera, excited now. "Perhaps We could use the meagre powers remaining to Us to help. Zeus can still conjure up the odd lightning bolt when He puts His mind to it."

Torsten shook his head, imagining arriving home with a group of well-meaning but work-shy, stunning but self-centred Gods and Goddesses in tow.

"No," he said firmly. "You are far too imposing and would only intimidate the person I have in mind."

"Very well," conceded Hera, "I will impart the good news to Zeus, and We can discuss this further tomorrow after the games."

She left him then, and he breathed a huge sigh of relief. He noticed that some of the slaves were now playing music and some dancing for their entertainment. Torsten gulped down a cup of wine and decided to go and show them how it was done.

The party continued into the early hours of the morning. Everyone was enjoying themselves so much that they didn't even notice BJ had gone.

CHAPTER FIVE

BJ's bewitchment

BJ had sneaked off as soon as he got the chance. He was desperately hoping to meet the bare-skinned beauty at the party, but she was nowhere to be seen, so he waited until everyone was engrossed in the concert on the rocks and then slipped into the shadows and found his way, by the light of the moons, to the pond where they had bathed only that morning.

As he reached the mossy bank at the side of the pond, he saw a figure moving in the shadows and quickly hid behind a tree. Peeping out, he recognised Artemis. She drew her bow, and seconds later, he heard a startled squawk. She briefly left his field of vision and promptly returned, holding the limp body of a large bird, which she stuffed unceremoniously into a bag, which she then swung back onto her shoulder.

"Come out, BJ," she said in a sing-song voice. "I know you're there."

He stepped out and said peevishly, "How did you know I was there? And what are you doing here anyway?"

"I'm a huntress," she said, "And also Goddess of the moon. There are two of them here, and they are almost at their fullness, so I am doubly restless. And anyway, I could ask you the same question, except that I already know the answer."

"I just fancied a swim," said BJ, deciding to bluff it out.

"You left a perfectly good party by the sea to come and swim in a pond?" said Artemis, laughing.

"I'm allergic to sea water," said BJ, feeling more and more foolish.

"Fair enough," said Artemis. "But talking of fair, the one you seek is not here. Hephaestus, her husband (BJ balked at this), keeps Her locked up at night to stop Her from escaping. She is only allowed out three times a day to bathe here, in this pond. And I am supposed to protect Her. But Aphrodite needs no protection. She can take care of Herself."

With that, she took up her bow again and strode off into the forest, leaving BJ to muse on what she had told him. So, this vision of beauty was married to the blacksmith. What a waste, he thought. He decided he didn't care; he just wanted to see her again. He sat down on the mossy bank and waited for dawn.

At first light, he was woken from a half-doze by the sound of splashing a way out in the pond. He stood, wincing with stiffness from sitting so long in the same position, slipped out of his robe and into the cool, fresh water.

He swam as quickly and quietly as he could to the rock where he had first spied the nubile nymph. She was not there but was near the far bank, washing herself in the shallow water. BJ could not hold back a gasp. She was even lovelier than he remembered, her long hair hanging in damp, golden skeins down her perfect back, water dripping in rivulets down the curves and contours of her beautiful body.

She looked up at the sound, her big, blue eyes wide with surprise, but then she seemed to relax when she saw who was there and continued her morning ablutions with calm composure and apparent indifference to BJ's presence. He hauled himself onto the rock where he had first seen her and watched, transfixed, unable to speak even if he had wanted to.

When she had finished, she stepped elegantly out of the pond, wiped herself with a cloth and walked away, turning once to regard him momentarily with a cool stare and a half-smile.

BJ thought that his heart was going to burst. She looked at me, he thought, and didn't send me away. He dived into the pond and swam back to the other end, where he clambered out and, still sopping wet and butt-naked, jumped up and down and waved his arms about, a joyful jig that even Torsten would have been proud of.

He was slightly less joyful when he got back to the beach to find it empty. As he trudged, exhausted from lack of sleep but elated from his early morning encounter with Aphrodite, up the mountain path and then up the steep stone staircase to the palace, he determined that he would go back to the pond that evening and that this time, he would speak.

CHAPTER SIX

The Olympic Games

"What happened to you, man?" asked Freki as BJ finally stumbled onto the terrace where his friends had just finished their breakfast. "I went into your room to wake you, but you weren't there."

"I went for a walk," said BJ and flopped into a chair.

A slave quickly came and brought fresh bread rolls, fruit and coffee. BJ accepted some coffee but was too exhausted to eat.

Torsten looked at him enquiringly.

BJ returned his look, grinned in spite of his tiredness and said, "So where are our magnanimous mountain dwellers? Still in bed?"

"Hmm, hmph," said Freki, finishing off a bread roll dripping with honey. "Bunch of lightweights. Can't hack the pace, man."

"I'm glad you're here, BJ," said Torsten a trifle gingerly.

He was paying the price for his overzealous partying of the night before and feeling slightly fragile.

"And I'm glad we're alone, as I want to talk to you all."

"You got a plan to get us out of here?" said Haakon. "About time."

He was feeling cranky because he had been escorted back to the palace under guard with the others and had not been permitted to spend the night with his beloved Calypso.

"Actually, yes," said Torsten. "I had a discussion with Hera yesterday evening, and I told her that there may be somebody in Traansylvania who could help them, but it would mean us going back there and dropping off the Bestefarians on the way."

"All the Bestefarians?" said Haakon.

"Well, Calpyso, obviously," said Torsten, "And as many of the others as we can fit on the Blomsthilda."

"Did you mean Petra, Uncle T?" said BJ, feeling slightly better after two cups of strong coffee. "Can she help them?"

"Well, no," admitted Torsten, "I don't believe she can, but the Theoi don't know that."

"But won' dey come after us when dey fin' out ya lied'?" asked Penelope.

"It's possible," said Torsten, massaging his sore temples. "But that's a risk we're going to have to take. Our first priority is to get everyone home safely."

"Ya, man," said Penelope.

"Cool," said Freki.

"Well done, Uncle T," said BJ. "Now, if you don't mind, I'm going to turn in for a while."

Haakon just grunted. They had some free time that morning before the mysterious games were due to begin in the afternoon, and he had been told that he would be allowed to see Calypso at lunchtime if he behaved himself, so he went to his room to do some warm-up exercises as he fancied his chances against Apollo, who he thought looked like a bit of a wimp.

Penelope wanted to get the story of the song written down while it was still fresh in her mind, so she politely asked one of the slaves for some ink and parchment and, as she scribbled, she translated it for Torsten, who used Bestefar's battered old notebook to jot down the translated version as best he could with the reed quill he'd been given. Freki got bored after a while and began fiddling with a board game he'd found inside in one of the rooms.

During a quick coffee break, Penelope said to Torsten, "Ya know it strange, Torsten, man. Da wife in da story was called Penelope, jus' like me."

Torsten thought about this for a while and then said, "Most of the Bestefarians have unusual names. None of them are Traansylvanian, so is it possible that when Anthe arrived in the Otherland, she started using names that she was familiar with in the language of this place?"

"Ya, man," nodded Penelope. "Dat mus' be it."

When they went back to their writing, Penelope paused and said, "Ah can' remember everytin' so well, an' ah wants to do dis justice, so ah tinks ah needs to talk to da Nereides and get a few detail straight. Can ya gimme some time to do dat, Torsten, man?"

Torsten nodded and said, "You know what, I'm not in a big hurry to leave. I quite like it here. So you take your time."

Penelope smiled gratefully and, after a moment of hesitation said, "Freki tol' me about what happen to ya, an' your frien' Kim, and … well … everytin'."

Torsten bit his lip, and his cheek twitched involuntarily.

"Ah'm truly sorry, Torsten, man," said Penelope softly. "Mebbe you can dedicate your version of da song to 'im. Ah'm goin' to dedicate mine to ma bestemor, Lidia."

"She'll love it," said Torsten hoarsely, and they got back to work.

Towards the end of the morning, Zeus ambled in. He smiled when he saw them.

"Well, aren't you all busy little bees?" he said. "A veritable hive of activity."

He glanced at Freki, who was toying idly with the beautifully carved figures on the game board.

"That's what We used to do with the humans," he chuckled, but when he saw the look on everyone's faces, he cleared his throat and said to Freki, "That's zatrikion, a long, tricky game but awfully good, so maybe if you fancy it some time…"

"Cool," said Freki.

He liked games. They heard the sound of a gong from somewhere inside the palace.

Hera came out, took Zeus's arm and said, "Time for a quick feast before you know what."

The long table in the banqueting hall was once again groaning with platters of food, and all the Gods and Goddesses had assembled, looking beautiful and cheerfully betting on who would win what. The only one absent was Haakon, who had been escorted down to the slave huts to eat with Calypso, as promised.

"You eat before the games?" said BJ, looking fresher now after his morning nap.

"Rather," said Apollo, chewing at the wing of some enormous bird that BJ suspected Artemis might have bagged the night before.

"We need to keep Our strength up, you know."

"We don't all play, though," said Hestia. "Poseidon does, but the rest of Us oldies sit it out and bet on the young ones."

Demeter nodded. Torsten realised he had never heard her speak and was wondering if she were mute.

"Di and I also sit it out," said Hermes, patting his enormous belly. "Only good at drinking games."

He and Dionysus clinked cups.

No sooner had they finished eating, Torsten and his team found themselves in the blink of an eye (or a clap of Zeus's hands in this case) on a vast, flat field, marked out into different playing areas. To one side on a raised plinth stood six thrones, on which were seated Zeus and Hera in the centre, with Hestia and Demeter on one side and Hermes and Dionysus on the other.

Haakon was already on the field, limbering up, but stopped when his teammates arrived to join them for the briefing, which was given by Hera, as Zeus was looking distinctly dozy after his meal.

Torsten was also tired. He asked Hera if he might also sit it out, given his age. She was about to say no, but Torsten did his jazz hands thing to remind her that he was also a God, or a minor deity at least, and the others obediently followed suit, so she relented, and another throne was placed for him at Hermes' side.

"Ya, man," he said to himself and sank gratefully into his seat.

Freki looked a bit peeved, and Torsten remembered that the young man preferred video games to actual physical activity.

"What's with the hands thing?" said Hermes, waggling his own in a fair imitation of Torsten's.

"Oh, just a thing we do," said Torsten.

"There will be five events that you will all compete in," announced Hera. "Long jump, javelin, discus, sprint and swimming. Men and women will compete separately."

Penelope breathed a sigh of relief, although she was still miffed that she was the only one in her team competing against Athena and Artemis.

"What about tennis?" asked Haakon, remembering the conversation from the previous night.

"No tennis," said Hera. "Since you were the only one in your team who said you could play, that hardly seemed fair."

"We can't do archery either," said Apollo, indicating his twin sister. "We're just too good at it."

"Or God at it," said Artemis, chuckling at her own joke.

Haakon grunted. He wasn't worried about Ares and Apollo, but even his well-toned physique was looking a little pathetic compared with the massive, rippling muscles of Poseidon and Hephaestus. BJ was also weighing Hephaestus up, but for an entirely different reason.

The games began, and took the rest of the afternoon to complete. Haakon did well in the throwing contests, BJ in the swimming, and Penelope actually gave the Goddesses a run for their money in the sprint. Poor old Freki didn't even get a look in, and it goes without saying that the Olympians came out on top in every event and wore their laurel wreaths triumphantly at the after-games feast that evening. Haakon had gone to have supper with Calypso, proudly clutching a bronze discus with which he had been presented by Zeus for his unexpected prowess in this discipline. He was tickled pink (reflected in his face) and was dying to show it off to her.

The Theoi were cheerful and garrulous at the feast, but Team Torsten was exhausted and ate and drank little. BJ was in a monumental sulk and scarcely spoke.

Freki tried to cheer him up by imitating Haakon after eating a lotus fruit, but his friend barely cracked a smile, and Torsten finally said, "Come on, BJ, you didn't seriously expect to win against a group of gargantuan Gods, did you?"

BJ got up huffily and said, "I'm going for a walk."

This provoked another arching of impeccable eyebrows, this time from Artemis, but nobody tried to stop him.

BJ's sulk had been partly real but partly put on because he knew that someone would lose patience with him in the end and give him the excuse he needed to storm out. He walked as quickly as he could, given the stiffness of his muscles after the games, down the stone stairs and followed the path all the way down to the pond. Artemis had said that Aphrodite was allowed out three times a day, and he was desperately hoping that he would catch her now. It was not too late, and although dusk was falling, it was still light enough to see.

He hastily disrobed and waded into the pond until it was deep enough to swim, careful not to splash or disturb the water too much. He kept deliberately to the outer edges of the pond and reached a conveniently situated rock behind which he could conceal himself and peek over the top to catch a glimpse of the object of his desire.

Aphrodite was indeed there on the rock where he had first seen and been enraptured by her. But she wasn't alone. Her lithe and lovely limbs were firmly wrapped around the beautifully sculpted body of a naked man with short, blond curls, shining with sweat.

"Ares," breathed BJ in disbelief.

The couple were moaning with pleasure, and BJ tasted bitterness in his mouth. He swam silently back to the shore, scooped up his discarded robe and managed to wait until he was under cover of the nearby trees to vomit up the small amount of food he'd consumed at the feast.

In the meantime, the feast had ended, and most of the Theoi and Penelope had drifted off to bed. Freki had been persuaded by Zeus to try a game of zatrikion, so Hera took Torsten by the arm and guided him out onto the terrace into the fresh, sweetly-scented night air.

"I know what you're going to ask," said Torsten, "and the answer is yes. I am going to try and help you. But as I said, I need to go home, and I want to drop the Bestefarians back at the Otherland, including, and this is very important, all those you took during your last raid, and as many of your other slaves who wish to leave the island."

Hera seemed taken aback by this.

"But how will We manage?" she asked. "We have so few slaves now as it is."

"You could try doing things by yourselves," suggested Torsten, but seeing Hera's shocked expression, he thought better of it and said, "Why don't you try the Bestefarian way? Give them freedom. Give them a choice. Who knows, some of them may decide to stay with you out of loyalty if they're no longer bound by servitude."

Hera didn't look convinced.

"You do want to get back to Earth, don't you?" said Torsten.

She pursed her lips and nodded.

"You drive a hard bargain, Bestefar," she said. "I will need to discuss this with Zeus. We will call a family conference tomorrow and let you know what We decide."

With that, she swept inside, and Torsten felt a huge wave of relief that that particular conversation was over and that he could now drag his weary, old bones to bed. Just watching the others competing had made him tired.

CHAPTER SEVEN

A family affair

The next morning after breakfast, Penelope went down to the beach to ask the Nereides to help her with the song. Haakon was no longer under guard and accompanied her on the pretext of going for a run, but secretly hoping to catch a glimpse of Calypso. Freki tried to interest BJ in a game of zatrikion, but he seemed preoccupied and was losing quite spectacularly. Torsten couldn't really settle to anything, as he knew that the family conference was taking place that morning, and he was anxious to hear the outcome. Eventually, tired of waiting, he wandered down to the beautiful, sheltered garden they had briefly passed through and sat on a stone bench, lost in memories.

He was roused from his reverie by Hera, who sat next to him on the bench. Torsten looked at her, waiting for her to speak first.

"It has been decided," she said. "We were not all entirely in agreement, but the prevailing wish is to go back to Earth, so We agree to your terms."

"All of them?" said Torsten, hardly believing his ear holes.

"All of them," she said. "We have already made an announcement to the slaves and, indeed, some of the older ones have decided to stay with Us."

She looked tired, Torsten thought. It must have taken some self-command to swallow her pride and change the habits of a very long lifetime.

"Thank you," he said.

"It had better be worth it," she said grimly. "When will you leave?"

Torsten thought for a moment.

"Penelope would like to finish her work on Homer," he said, "but we can only fit ourselves and those you took recently from the Otherland on the Blomsthilda, so we need to find a way to transport the others."

Hera gave him a haughty 'you should have thought of that before' kind of look, and Torsten felt a bit sheepish.

"We did have a fleet of small ships," said Hera, but they have all fallen sadly into disrepair, and none would be big enough to hold so many."

"I will find a solution," said Torsten with a confidence he didn't really feel, "for I am Bestefar."

Hera seemed to accept this, and with a sudden clap of her hands, they were back in the banqueting hall for the midday feast. Everyone else was already there and seemed pleased to see him, although this was most probably because they were waiting for him before they could begin eating. Penelope, however, seemed genuinely pleased to see him and told him that her visit to the Nereides had been most productive and that she should be able to finish writing easily in a few days. This cheered Torsten up mightily after his difficult conversation with Hera, and that, combined with his walk down to the garden, gave him a hearty appetite for the feast before him.

That afternoon, Penelope returned to the beach to pick the Hereides' beautiful brains again, and for want of something better to do, Torsten accompanied her. He was delighted to see that Hermes and Dionysus were sitting side by side on matching deckchairs with an enormous pitcher of wine on a table between them. They greeted him like a long-lost friend and brought him a chair and a cup, which he felt obliged to accept, although he was not wont to drink in the afternoon.

They had a whale of a time; Hermes regaling him with stories of when he was messenger to the Gods and Torsten sharing tales of the theatre with Dionysus. He didn't notice the time passing until he heard the familiar sound of the conch shell and realised that another bout of sea polo was about to commence. Penelope came to join them as the Nereides were preparing to play, and she was also given a chair and plied with wine.

"My bet's on the girls today," boomed Dionysus, helping himself to another cup of wine.

"How about you, Herm?" But Hermes was fast asleep.

Dionysus smiled indulgently and settled himself deeper in his deckchair as the match began. Torsten was feeling quite mellow after a few glasses of wine and enjoying the athletic grace of the creatures flipping in and out of the water, when he had a brainwave. When they got back to the palace and he had bathed in cold water to clear his head, he caught Hera and Zeus before the evening feast, and they went out onto the terrace together.

"I've had an idea," said Torsten, his face pink from excitement and his cold bath. "Could we use the dolphiniums to carry the additional slaves?"

"Slaves no longer," said Zeus.

Torsten couldn't gauge from the old man's expression whether he was happy about this or not.

"Bestefarians, then," Torsten corrected. "What do you think? Is it possible?"

"It can be done," said Hera, nodding thoughtfully. "Poseidon could accompany them to keep the sea creatures in check, and I think Hermes could do with some exercise. He is our messenger, after all, and could carry a message of peace and goodwill to your people."

"That's settled then," said Zeus. "Come, let us celebrate."

Torsten was thrilled. Zeus made the announcement over dinner, having to translate it subsequently. Calypso was there and was so happy she kissed Haakon full on the lips, causing more eyebrow-raising among their hosts, leading Freki to wonder if this might not be a potential new Olympic sport.

"Well, there's no point in the girl continuing her training," said Hera, quelling the eyebrow-raising. "She's a free … erm …" She hesitated.

"Person," said BJ.

He hadn't spoken for some time, and Torsten smiled at him.

"Precisely," said Hera.

BJ stood up.

"I'm going with them," he announced.

Freki expressed everyone's surprise by saying, "Why, man?"

BJ had been feeling truly terrible after what he had seen at the pond; disappointed, disgusted and, in all honesty, desperate to avoid having to do something about the situation, like telling Hephaestus that his wife was having a torrid affair with Ares, whose name was an anagram of "arse", he suddenly realised with a small sense of satisfaction. Also, he really liked the idea of riding a dolphinium.

What he actually said was, "It makes sense. As soon as I reach the Otherland, I can contact Aunty D and give her an update. They must all be really worried."

"That's brilliant, BJ," said Torsten, doing his jazz hands thing, which meant that everyone else also had to follow suit.

"You'll be the advance guard. You can give everyone the good news and tell them that we'll follow shortly on the Blomsthilda."

"Ahem," said Hermes. "I get to make the announcement, though, right?"

He was excited at the prospect of getting his old job back, and equally excited at the prospect of riding a dolphinium, though he hoped they would find him a good sturdy one that could take his weight.

"Yeah, of course," said BJ. "I'll just be your wingman."

It wasn't until everyone started laughing that he understood his unintentional joke.

Hera called Xenia over and said, "Tell everyone to make ready for tomorrow. The moons are waning, and We don't want to miss the high tides."

"Tell them yourself," said Xenia cheerfully. "I'm off to pack."

CHAPTER EIGHT

Demeter's diatribe

Next morning's exodus was quite an emotional affair. The newly freed slaves who had decided to stay lined up on the beach to bid farewell to those who were leaving, and Freki was inconsolable after BJ had hugged them all (even Haakon) and mounted his dolphinium. He waved cheerfully enough, however, as the curious convoy struck out into the bay with Poseidon leading the way, riding his giant eel and brandishing his trident like a tour guide with an umbrella, and Hermes lagging behind, desperately trying not to fall off his poor, put-upon dolphinium.

"May Bestefar be wid ya," said Penelope, waving back.

"Ya, man," responded the others, apart from Freki, who was crying too much to be able to speak.

They stayed and watched until the seafarers were swallowed by the horizon, and Freki's sobs had subsided to an intermittent snuffle.

The days passed smoothly and uneventfully after that. Torsten and Penelope continued their writing, and Freki moped around a lot, missing BJ and playing the occasional game of zatrikion with Zeus when he wasn't playing golf. Haakon had started spending a lot of time playing tennis with Ares. He was also teaching

Calypso to play, and occasionally, they would have a game of doubles with Ares and Athena.

Ares had had plenty of experience with the vagaries of human nature and the metaphysical battle between good and evil. He was the God of war, after all. Ares could sense a deep-rooted conflict in Haakon and had also detected animosity from BJ before he left. Not dissimilar to humans, this race, he thought, and decided it was time to have a little fun.

He pumped Haakon's already over-inflated ego, praising him for his sporting skills and even letting him win the odd tennis match here and there. Haakon had been feeling a bit bad about what he had done in Traansylvania, but Ares made him feel good about himself again. He constantly encouraged him to think that he was superior to the others and that he deserved better. It wasn't long before Haakon started believing him, believing in himself again, and was looking for an opportunity to show everyone that his name, Haakon, "the chosen one", actually meant something.

Hermes and Poseidon had returned safely from their mission, having duly returned the Bestefarians to their homeland and delivered their message of peace to Lidia, whose initial terror of the two giant Gods had turned to relief and gratitude when she heard what they and BJ had to tell her. She had sent her love and told them to "get deir backsides back home before she got really cross, now man."

One afternoon about a week after their return, as Penelope's book was nearing completion, Torsten was taking a well-earned break and sauntered down to his favourite spot in the garden. It gave welcome shade from the mid-afternoon heat and also gave Torsten the impression of being closer to Kim somehow. He had grown used to seeing Demeter occasionally pottering about in the garden, but they had never disturbed each other; he leaving her to her gardening, and she leaving him to his quiet contemplation.

Today, however, he was surprised to see her approaching him. She put down the watering vessel she was carrying and indicated the bench, asking his permission to sit.

"Please," said Torsten, shifting up slightly on the bench.

"You really don't need to ask."

Demeter smiled and sat. She cleared her throat.

"Hello," she said timidly.

"Hello, Demeter," said Torsten, surprised and pleased to discover that she could speak after all.

"Oh, you know My name?" she said, putting her hand over her mouth in wonder.

"How very kind you are. And you are Bestefar?"

"Well, actually, it's Torsten," said Torsten.

"I wanted to talk to you, Torsten," said Demeter. "I've been waiting to pluck up the courage."

"Oh, what about?" asked Torsten, his face as green as the vine leaves above them with curiosity.

"About Them," replied Demeter, jerking her head in the direction of the palace.

"Your family?" said Torsten, frowning slightly.

"My family," spat Demeter suddenly, taking Torsten completely off guard, "are a bunch of conniving, incestuous toads."

"Wha… what?" spluttered Torsten.

"You have no idea what They're capable of," said Demeter. "You have walked into a nest of vipers, and you need to get out as soon as you can before it's too late."

"What do you mean?" asked Torsten, his complexion now fluctuating between a series of colours that competed with the wide variety of succulent fruits hanging from the branches around them. "I don't understand. Why are you telling me this?"

"Your man Haakon is spending too much time with Ares for a start," she said. "He is the God of war, violence and bloodshed. He was born to be trouble. Not somebody I would really recommend as a friend."

Torsten nodded. But Demeter was far from done.

"You know that He's also banging Aphrodite, Hephaestus' wife, don't you?" she said.

"Haakon?" squeaked Torsten.

"No, Ares, the randy goat," said Demeter. "They're all randy goats, actually. All banging each other. Apart from Hestia and Athena. They're alright."

"I didn't even know Hephaestus had a wife," said Torsten, his mind boggling.

"He keeps her locked up most of the time," said Demeter. "She has secret trysts with Ares at Her pond and Artemis, who's supposed to 'protect' Her, turns a blind eye."

"But how can they all be banging each other?" said Torsten, totally confused now. "Aren't you all related?"

"The Theoi are not good role models for society as a whole," said Demeter. "Incest is rife. Zeus will bang anything in a skirt, male or female, or used to before His divine dick shrivelled with age. He's forced himself on Me more than once, and Poseidon's just as bad. Not to mention wet and slimy."

"But they're your brothers," wailed Torsten, his voice getting more and more shrill in direct proportion to the gravity of Demeter's revelations.

And then the final nail in the coffin of his idealistic illusions.

"You do know Hera's His sister, as well as his wife, don't you?" said Demeter with a kind of cruel satisfaction. "That's why she hates Me so much."

"Enough!" said Torsten, his head reeling.

He stood up quickly and half-ran, half-stumbled out of the garden. Demeter watched him leave with tears in her eyes.

"I just thought he should know," she said to no one in particular.

CHAPTER NINE

The calm before the storm

Penelope's Homer-based opus was finally finished, and she was very pleased with it. She had run it by the Nereides, who had clapped and waggled their tails appreciatively. Torsten had thrown himself into his own version with single-minded determination. After his agony in the garden with Demeter, he hadn't been able to bring himself to tell the others what he had learned. He had since avoided Demeter and the garden and tried to behave normally towards the other Theoi, repressing his sense of revulsion and focusing on preparing for their departure.

He had taken it upon himself, however, to speak to Calypso in private. He tried to warn her, in the nicest possible way, that Ares might not be having the best influence on Haakon and that maybe he should spend a little less time with him. But Calypso was deeply in love, and although she nodded and promised Torsten she would keep an eye on the situation, she went straight to Haakon and told him what Torsten had said. He was furious.

"That interfering old drittbag," he growled.

He took Calypso in his arms.

"Cali, my own goddess," he said, "nobody takes me seriously. I'm a computer hacker turned PE teacher. I was destined for greater things and have been thwarted at every turn. I have a cunning plan, however, that will make us rich beyond our wildest dreams and put my name in the history books forever."

He outlined his plan to Calypso.

"You is so clever an' greater dan a god to me, ma love," she breathed. "What can ah do to help?"

"First, we need to find out where everyone is," said Haakon.

It was early afternoon, and the Theoi were nowhere to be seen. Now that Penelope had finished her book, she was spending more time with Freki, and he was teaching her to play zatrikion. Torsten had taken to spending the afternoon in his room, avoiding everyone and scribbling frantically. He was particularly avoiding Hera, at whom he couldn't bear to look and who was dropping heavier and heavier hints now about them leaving.

"I need you to distract Torsten," he whispered to Calypso, "Get him out of the palace for a while."

Calypso racked her brain to think of something that might tempt Torsten out of his hidey-hole. She knocked tentatively at the door of his room. There was no answer, so she knocked louder. The door opened a crack and then opened fully as Torsten saw who it was.

"Calypso," he said. He looked relieved. "Is everything alright?"

"Ah's had an argument wi' Haakon 'bout what ya said," she lied. "Ah's wantin' to go for a walk down to da beach. Get away from him for a while and get some fresh air. Tought mebbe ya like to come wid me and tell me more 'bout dis homeless guy?"

"Homer," corrected Torsten, smiling.

Why the dritt not, he thought. He could also do with some fresh air and exercise. His book was almost finished, and he was tired of being cooped up. Besides, he enjoyed Calypso's company and couldn't help thinking she was wasted on Haakon.

They walked companionably down to the beach, and Torsten showed her Homer's tomb and told her all he had learned about him from Zeus. Calypso nodded and smiled and wondered inwardly how soon she could politely escape.

In the meantime, Haakon briefly visited Penelope's room and saw the pile of parchments covered in indecipherable symbols sitting on a table. Perfect, he thought. From there, he entered Torsten's room and quickly located the battered notebook Torsten had been using to write in. He flicked through the contents, and his attention was caught by the last chapter, which was not Homer's work. Torsten had taken it upon himself to write an honest account of the Theoi; their innate cruelty and their incestuous proclivities. Haakon was thrilled; this was exactly what he needed and even better than he had hoped.

"Ares," he whistled appreciatively, "You sly old sneglhund!"

Calypso thanked Torsten politely when they finally reached the top of the stone staircase and entered the cool entrance hall of the palace. He went back to his room to freshen up before the evening feast, and she went straight to Haakon, who told her what he had discovered in Torsten's book.

She was shocked at first, but Haakon cupped her beautiful face in his hands and said, "This is it, Cali, baby. Our ticket out of here. Put your sacred hat back on and hold onto it because we are going on a trip."

After the evening feast, Torsten stood up and said, "I have an announcement."

Everyone looked at him expectantly.

"We are leaving the day after tomorrow," he said, avoiding the gaze of the Theoi and ignoring the surprise of his companions.

"It is time."

"Very well," rumbled Zeus, "You will have fair winds and tides, and the creatures of the sea will give you no trouble."

Hera nodded and smiled graciously, fairly pointlessly, since Torsten refused to meet her eye.

"Thank you," said Torsten and promptly left the room.

"Is he alright?" whispered Freki to Penelope, who shrugged and said, "Ah don' know, Freki man. Mebbe he missin' BJ. But ah's jus' so glad we is goin' home."

Haakon whispered to Calypso, "That's sooner than I thought. Tomorrow, we make our move."

CHAPTER TEN

Trouble strikes again

Haakon was up early and, unusually, on the golf course with Zeus. He had never shown the slightest interest in golf, but Zeus seemed content to have someone to whom he could show the ropes and show off.

As they pootled around the very pleasant course, Haakon flattered Zeus on his better shots (of which, frankly, there were few; he was a mediocre player for a God) and asked him a lot of questions about himself, which also pleased Zeus as He (aside from golf) was his favourite subject of conversation. Haakon expertly steered the conversation around to the fateful day of the storm that had literally moved a mountain. Zeus looked unbearably sad as he recalled the events of that day.

"If there are greater gods than Us," he said, "then I suppose this could be considered a suitable punishment on their part for Our hubris."

Haakon decided it was too early in the morning for philosophy and didn't respond. Instead, he looked up to the palace perching precariously on the mountainside.

"So you were up there when it happened?" he asked.

"Indeed," said Zeus. "I was looking out from the big balcony up there. The Titans were camped on the top of Mount Orthrys and were about to launch another attack. I was growing frightfully weary of the war and decided it was time to end it once and for all. I summoned a terrible storm and the most mighty lightning bolt I could muster. By some curious twist of fate or freak of nature (Haakon did note at this point that he was still reluctant to accept the blame), the bolt struck Us instead, and the rest, as they say, is history."

Haakon smiled.

"Easier than taking candy from a baby," he thought, and then excused himself, saying he had a terrible headache and needed to lie down.

"Nice chap," thought Zeus as he watched him leave. "Terrible at golf, though."

Haakon spent the rest of the day with Calypso making ready. Hera had announced at the midday feast that they would be having an even bigger and better farewell feast that evening. Torsten patted his paunch and thought that it was a very good thing they were leaving tomorrow before he started looking like Hermes. He was in a better mood and very much looking forward to getting back to the Otherland, and then finally home to Traansylvania. He didn't dare think about whether Arne was still alive. He desperately wanted to see his old friend and tell him all about their amazing adventures. He spent the afternoon putting the final touches to his book.

The farewell feast was quite a jolly affair. Hephaestus had been persuaded to let Aphrodite out for the evening, and she caused quite a stir, not only because of her breathtaking beauty but because none of the non-Theoi had ever seen her, and other than Torsten and BJ, of course, didn't even know she existed.

She was fully clothed and looked sensational in a long, white silk robe, and Ares wasn't the only one who couldn't take his eyes off her. Hephaestus looked huffy and sat her firmly between himself and Hera. She was silent but smiled a lot and seemed genuinely pleased to be there.

Freki smacked his forehead.

"Aphrodite's pond, man," he said. "We swam there."

Aphrodite shot him a look, and Freki gulped. He suddenly felt like his entire body had just been immersed in scalding hot water. He hastily gulped some wine. Dionysus had really pulled out all the stops, or stoppers, in this case, for the last supper. Torsten had thoroughly enjoyed discussing theatre things with him and complimented him on the wine, telling him truthfully that it was the best he'd ever tasted and that his mouth felt like it was in Heaven.

Dionysus bowed in acknowledgement and said, "Elysium."

Torsten gave him a blank look, wondering if this meant "thank you" in their language, but Dionysus grinned and said, "Elysium. It's what We call Heaven; the abode of the blessed after death."

The feast continued, and a great deal of the wonderful wine was consumed. When Hebe and the slaves, who were now servants, started clearing the table, throwing the meat bones to the massive, three-headed dog, who growled its thanks in triplicate, everyone retired to the colonnaded terrace with the beautiful vista of the island and the pink sea beyond.

"So Torsten," began Haakon, who had drunk only water all evening on the pretext that his headache of the morning was still bothering him, "wouldn't you like to read us all a bit of your book before we leave."

"Erm …," said Torsten. "No … err … why?"

"You've been working so hard on it," said Haakon. "Surely you'd like us to hear the fruit of your labours."

"Not lotus fruit, though, right man?" said Freki with a giggle.

Haakon chose to ignore this and continued, "Particularly that last chapter with all the juicy details about our hosts here, and what they get up to behind closed doors, or in ponds," he added, with a meaningful look at Aphrodite, whose frown did nothing to diminish her devastating loveliness.

"You read it?" said Torsten with the high-pitched squeak he was rapidly turning into an art form.

Haakon smugly patted the bag he was wearing across his chest and which nobody had noticed up to this point.

"I have it right here," he said.

Torsten was about to make a grab for it, but he was stopped in his tracks by Zeus, who, in anger, appeared to have recaptured some of his former grandeur, shouting in a booming voice which almost knocked Torsten off his feet, "What is the meaning of this? What book? What juicy details?"

"It's fascinating reading," said Haakon, noting with satisfaction the freshening wind and the uneasy calls of the sea birds.

"Quite the bonk-buster. Should be a real hit back home. Has all the ingredients: mystery, charisma, power struggles, passion, hate, love, clandestine affairs ..."

"How dare you?" screamed Hera. "We have given you hospitality, treated you like royalty, and this is how you repay Us?"

"What clandestine affairs?" growled Hephaestus, pushing Hera unceremoniously aside and standing before Haakon like a monolith with muscles.

"Wow, man," thought Freki. "He makes Haakon look like a sneglhund pup."

"Oh, you didn't know?" said Haakon with infuriating sang-froid.

"Maybe you should ask Ares. Or your *wife*," he added, with extra emphasis on the last word.

Hephaestus turned around and lifted Ares clean off the floor as if he were picking up a child and started shaking him. Aphrodite ran over to him and beat at him ineffectually with her fists. Everyone was so busy watching this that they didn't notice the dark clouds forming and the waves foaming in the bay below.

"Oh yes, plenty of sex," continued Haakon. "And then the incest..."

All eyes turned to him at this point, and Hephaestus dropped Ares like an unwanted doll. The thought crossed Ares's mind briefly that this wasn't really what he had bargained for when he began stirring up trouble, just before he lost consciousness.

"Ho yuss," said Haakon, really enjoying himself now. "Brothers and sisters, getting it on. Did you know that your husband raped your sister, Hera?"

Hera was seething with rage. Freki had a sudden vision of fangs and a head writhing with serpents in place of hair. He shuddered.

"And that's when Poseidon here wasn't having a bash at her," Haakon indicated Demeter, who was standing open-mouthed with her hands crossed in horror over her crepey breasts.

There was a distant rumble of thunder from somewhere out at sea. Zeus approached Haakon, fury traced in every line of his wizened face.

"I think that's quite enough, young man," he said.

It couldn't have sounded more threatening if he'd said he was about to remove his testicles and turn them into golf balls.

But Haakon hadn't quite finished. He took Calypso's hand and retreated to the far end of the terrace, leaning against the balustrade. The wind was now whipping at their robes, and Haakon had to yell to make himself heard over the violent squalls and the thunderous crashing of the waves.

"And I'm pretty sure they've all had a go at your wife here, don't you think so, old man?" shouted Haakon scornfully at Zeus.

He was reaching his apotheosis.

"Or should I say your SISTER?"

"I warned you," cried Zeus, raising his arms to the broiling skies above.

"Nooooooo," screamed Hera, trying to reach him, but she was too late.

A blinding streak of light shot from his hands and hit Haakon and Calypso full-on, sending them tumbling out into the stormy darkness.

Everything suddenly went quiet, bar a few sparks still hissing on the handrail before fizzling out.

"Holy dritt!" said Freki.

Penelope ran up to Torsten, out of breath. He hadn't noticed that she had disappeared during the kerfuffle.

"Torsten, man, ma book ... it gone," she said, tears pouring down her bluish-tinged face.

"So have Haakon and Calypso," said Torsten, just before Zeus crumpled heavily to the ground.

CHAPTER ELEVEN

Now you Elysium, now you don't

In the summer of 1947, Herbert Miller, more commonly known as Herb, was doing the daily tour of his ranch in southeastern New Mexico. He was especially concerned about one particular pasture, wanting to make sure that his ranch hands had mended the fence, damaged in a recent storm, as he'd asked.

As he rode, he felt the familiar tingle he always felt when he crossed an energy pathway. His father, Heinrich Müller, was born to German immigrants in Minneapolis in the early 1900s. In 1920, he followed the example of many of his young friends and moved to Los Angeles in search of work. He fell in love with and married a certain Frieda Schmidt, who worked in a natural food restaurant in downtown LA called The Eutropheon. She was part of a movement that espoused natural living and "lebensreform" or life-reform, as it was known. At the outset of the 1960s, these ageing "nature boys" served as role models for the rebellious youth that would later become known as "hippies".

Heinrich's name, like many of his compatriots', got transposed over time to the more manageable Henry Miller. He and Frieda had a son, Herbert, and decided on a complete lifestyle change, swapping their urban existence in Los Angeles for a simpler life on a cattle ranch out in the sticks in New Mexico.

Frieda adored nature and was a deeply spiritual person. She would take the young Herbert out divining with a hazel rod and tell him all about the energy pathways that criss-cross the Earth. She was delighted to discover that her son had a mystical gift and could feel the power in a way that she had never been able to.

On this particular June morning, as Herb felt the familiar prickling of the hairs on the back of his neck, he felt something else: a peculiar pulsing sensation in his head as if a band were tightening around his skull. He felt dizzy and dismounted from his horse, who also seemed on edge, whickering uneasily and tossing her mane.

The grass in the middle of the prairie in which he was standing had been flattened. As he got closer, he saw a small crater in the centre of the grass, which was slightly singed around the edges and almost gagged when he realised that what was lying in the crater was a body. On closer examination, the body appeared to be covered in scorch marks, and its skull had been cracked open, the unsightly gash almost invisible beneath the swarm of flies busily feasting on the dried blood caked around it. It was wearing what was left of a charred and blood-splattered robe that might once have been white. The four unseeing eyes indicated that it was definitely not human. A few feet from the body lay a battered, metallic disc engraved with concentric circles.

"Well, I'll be darned," said Herb, not quite believing what he was seeing.

"I think Sheriff Wilcox might wanna see this."

Haakon had taken a calculated risk. Despite knowing little about the technology behind the bracelet with which Petra had sent him to the Otherland, he had asked Hephaestus to delicately cut the stone in two and set one half in a metallic bracelet similar to his own. He had hoped that he and Calypso might end up either back there, or in Traansylvania.

His plan had been to steal the books and get to Traansylvania before the others, sell the contents and show that stuck-up journalist Lise Lauritsen that he wasn't a fraud and that he was capable of giving her a sensational scoop, making himself famous in the process.

When he landed, half-blinded, frazzled and winded from the impact, he looked around in panic, realising with horror that neither Calypso nor the bag he had been carrying were in the vicinity. He called Calypso's name weakly, but there was no response. As his vision cleared, he looked up into the cloudless, blue sky above him and heaved a shaky sigh of relief. At least he was still alive.

The last thing he saw, careering towards him at breakneck speed and glistening in the sunlight, was a large, circular, metal disc, before the sunlight exploded in front of his eyes, and everything went black.

CHAPTER TWELVE

There's no place like Homer

Zeus was propped up in bed on a mountain of pillows when Torsten, Freki and Penelope went to say their goodbyes. He looked older and smaller somehow.

"I'm sorry about your friends," he wheezed.

"Haakon wasn't really a friend," said Torsten. "And Calypso ... well ... she loves him and would follow him to the ends of the universe, which is possibly where they are right now."

"How is it possible, though?" asked Zeus. "Did he have powers too?"

"He had something very special that the person I was telling you about used to transport him from my home to the Otherland," said Torsten.

"Why couldn't We have used it then?" asked Hera. "You could have sent Us back to Earth."

She looked sad rather than angry, Torsten thought.

"It doesn't work like that," he replied. "To be perfectly honest, I don't really know how it works. I lost the device that set it off when I was transported to the

Otherland, so I honestly didn't think it would work any more. But Haakon is clever. He knew that all it needed was a massive electrical charge, which you provided."

"I said I was sorry," said Zeus, slightly peevishly.

He really wasn't feeling very well.

"It wasn't your fault," said Torsten. "He provoked you deliberately. He knew exactly what he was doing."

"That poor excuse for a mortal has a bad case of hubris," croaked Zeus. "Not to mention kleos."

"Yes, but in his defence," said Hera, who had evidently not entirely got over her crush on Haakon, "he also had thumos in abundance."

Torsten didn't understand any of this but hoped whatever it was might be fatal. Hera now turned her attention to him.

"Is it true about what you wrote?" she asked.

"Yes," admitted Torsten. "I needed to get it all down … out of my system if you like."

"I don't like," said Hera. "I do not relish the thought of Our dirty laundry being washed out there somewhere."

"I doubt if anyone would believe it anyway," said Torsten, with the ghost of a smile.

"Can we go now, Torsten man?" said Penelope.

"Yes, I think we're done here," said Torsten.

"Cool," said Freki.

Hera clapped her hands, and they found themselves back on the beach where they had first met Zeus. Torsten was delighted to see the Blomsthilda still floating a little way out in the bay. Hermes and Dionysus had turned out to see them off, together with the servants who had agreed to stay behind.

As Freki and Penelope pushed the rowing boat back out into the surf, Hera said to Torsten, "Farewell Bestefar. Don't forget your promise."

"I won't," said Torsten, hoping she wouldn't notice that he had his fingers crossed behind his back.

He waded through the waves, and Freki helped him into the boat. The Bestefarians who had been captured rode next to them on dolphiniums. As they passed the headland, the Nereides waved at them. They were singing a different song this time.

"Dey sayin' goodbye," said Penelope with tears in her eyes.

As Torsten looked back towards the shore, he was astonished to see that everyone, even Hera, was doing his jazz hands thing. He did it back, his vision clouding with unexpected emotion as they boarded the Blomsthilda.

Freki took the helm, and Torsten helped Penelope unfurl the sails. The winds were as fair as Zeus had promised, and they set off at a good lick. Soon, they were in open seas once more, and Torsten breathed a huge sigh of relief.

"Thank the Gods for that," he said.

"Not those Gods, though?" said Freki.

"Helvete no," said Torsten with feeling. "Although," he said after a brief pause, "I wonder if our Gods, Odin and his lot, were any better."

Freki shrugged, and Penelope joined him at the helm, putting her arms around him. The rest of the voyage passed in relative silence. The Bestefarians didn't like the motion of the boat, and they were also very subdued because of Calypso's sudden and unexplained disappearance. They were hoping that they may find her safe and sound on the island upon their return.

As they approached the Otherland, they saw an excited crowd waiting for them on the beach, and as they got closer, they could just make out Lidia, Sophia and BJ right at the front, waving frantically.

"No sign of Haakon or Calypso," said Torsten.

With no dolphiniums to help, they had to make two trips with the rowing boats to get everyone to shore. Torsten and Freki went first with a small group of Bestefarians and then returned for Penelope and the others. There was a great deal of hugging and some tears, and once they had established that Haakon and Calypso had not re-appeared on the island in a puff of smoke, Lidia summarily dismissed the welcoming committee and packed Torsten, Freki and Penelope off to bathe and rest.

"We'll 'ave a proper catch-up at dinner," she said, smiling her toothless smile.

Torsten asked BJ to accompany him to his hut. As soon as they were inside, they both started asking questions simultaneously.

"Sorry, you first, Uncle T," said BJ.

"How's Dordi?" asked Torsten.

"She's fine," said BJ. "Dying to see you, obviously."

The word "dying" gave Torsten the shivers.

"And Arne," he asked, closing his eyes and dreading the response.

"He's still alive," said BJ. "Aunty D told me he categorically refused to die until you got back."

Torsten smiled.

"That sounds like Arne," he said.

"So what happened after I left?" said BJ. "Where are Haakon and Calypso?"

Torsten gave him a potted version of events, and BJ's four eyes gradually grew wider and wider.

"What a drittsek! And you thought they might have ended up here?" he said, once Torsten had finished.

"Yes," said Torsten. "There was a good chance. But they could be anywhere. They could be in Traansylvania for all we know."

"Shall we find out?" said BJ, taking his phone out of the pouch he had tied around his waist.

"Yes, please," said Torsten.

Never had he been so pleased to see his sister's face.

"Dordi," he almost yelled. "It's so good to see you!"

Dordi looked slightly haggard, but her face was pink with pleasure.

"Torsten," she said. "Are you coming home?"

"I'll be there soon, sis," he said. "Erm … have you heard anything about Haakon, by any chance?"

"Haakon?" she squealed, doing a fairly good impression of her brother.

"That drittbag? Don't tell me he's up to his old tricks again."

"I'm afraid so," said Torsten with a sigh.

"You would know if he was in Traansylvania, I think. He would have arrived in a blaze of glory, or a blaze of lightning in this case."

"I can ask Petra," said Dordi. "Although I'm pretty sure she would have told me or Elea if she'd heard anything."

"She would have called me already," said BJ., "But yeah, ask her to call us if she knows anything."

"Will do," said Dordi. "And please hurry back. I don't know if Arne can hold on much longer. He's dying to see you."

She cringed visibly at what she had just said.

"Tell him to hang on in there," said Torsten.

He blew his sister a kiss and hung up.

BJ left Torsten then. They met up again at dinner. Penelope had already filled her mother and grandmother in on everything that had happened, and BJ had received a call from his mother, who knew as little as Dordi about Haakon's whereabouts.

Over a pipeful of kaya, for which Torsten was extremely grateful, Lidia thanked them profusely for freeing the slaves, and they discussed what should happen next.

Penelope lamented the loss of her book but said that every word was engraved in her memory and that, following the oral tradition of the bards, she would teach it to the Bestefarians. Torsten was also upset about the loss of his opus, particularly as it had been written in Bestefar's precious notebook, but he said that he could also remember most of it and could rewrite it when he got back home if he felt up to it.

"I 'as ta say dat dem Theoi soun' like a right bunch o' bad news," said Lidia. "Aldough da chubby one dat come 'ere was kinda cute."

"Ya, man," said Sophia.

"Do ya tink dey goin' to cause us problems if dey don' hear from ya?" she asked Torsten.

"I think Zeus is dying," said Torsten. "I don't know how that will affect things, but they may have other things on their minds for a while."

"An' if Haakon does turn up?" said Lidia, puffing on her pipe.

"We'll cross that bridge when we come to it," said Torsten. "In the meantime, I'm ready to go home."

"Me too," said BJ. "I can't wait to get back to my nice, comfy office. How about you, Frek?"

He looked at Freki, who looked like he would like to hide under the table. Penelope took his hand and gave it a reassuring squeeze.

"You're not coming back, are you?" said BJ, with a catch in his voice.

"I wanna stay here with Penelope, man," said Freki. "I'm sorry BJ."

He looked like he was going to cry.

"Hey, it's cool, man", said BJ. "You're only a boat ride away, after all."

"Well, that's settled then," said Torsten. "We leave tomorrow on the morning tide."

CHAPTER THIRTEEN

Calypso

Calypso awoke alone and dazed on a beach, her head ringing. She called out for Haakon, but there was no reply. She lay on the warm sand with the waves lapping at her legs for some time, until she felt sufficiently recovered to get up and have a look around. It took her a long time to reluctantly accept that she was totally, completely and utterly on her own.

It could have been worse. The island where she found herself was large and had plentiful provisions of food and fresh water.

Occasionally, she would walk up to the palace on the mountain and wander around the large, empty rooms, talking to imaginary people and holding imaginary feasts at the vast, marble-topped table.

She also spent a lot of time on the deserted beach. At first, she would look out for passing boats, but she never saw a single one. There were some boats on the island, but they were completely dilapidated with age and no longer seaworthy. Calypso was also deeply afraid of the water; particularly this water.

She was convinced that Haakon would come and find her eventually. And so she sat for hours on end at her favourite vantage point at the foot of a cliff, next to an ancient stone monument and a group of more recent graves, looking out to sea, waiting and hoping.

And it was there that she died, alone and bereft, still hoping and dreaming of happier times with her beloved Haakon.

CHAPTER FOURTEEN

The return of the heroes

It was another emotional farewell on the shore of the Otherland as a much smaller band of unlikely heroes consisting of Torsten and BJ prepared to make their way home. To sweeten the pill and in an attempt to stem Freki's tears, which threatened to cause a dangerous rise in salt water levels, Torsten had promised that he would bring the family over to see the Bestefarians as soon as he could.

Lidia kissed them both on the forehead, saying, "May Bestefar be wid ya."

"Ya, man," they chanted fervently together with the crowd who had come to see them off.

And this time, BJ didn't wipe it away.

After an uneventful journey, they swung into the small harbour in Columbia Bay, where Bestefar had hidden the Blomsthilda. An ecstatic welcoming committee was waiting for them on the quay: Elea, Jan, Petra and Sander with a sleeping Annette in his arms, all waving frantically and almost smothering them with hugs as soon as they crossed the gangplank.

"Sorry Mamma couldn't come," said Elea. "She can't leave Pappa alone right now."

"How is he?" asked Torsten.

"Weak," said Elea. "But he rallied a little this morning when he heard you were coming home."

They walked up to Bestefar's cottage and quickly ate the picnic lunch Dordi had prepared for them. It was the first time Torsten had seen Annette, and his heart melted as he bounced the bonny baby girl on his knee. Then they walked to Bestefar's grave, pristine again with a brand new headstone, to pay their respects, and also to Petra Senior and dear old Sven and Cookie, buried nearby.

"I lost his notebook," said Torsten, turning a sorrowful shade of blue.

"You didn't lose it, Uncle T," said BJ. "That son of a dritt, Haakon, stole it."

Torsten nodded.

"True. Still no sign of him?" he asked.

BJ shook his head.

"I even asked Lise," he said. "I thought she'd be the first person he'd contact if he was back here, but she said she hadn't heard from him and sincerely hoped that she never would. Ever again. Ever."

He chuckled.

"Are you two alright then?" asked Torsten.

"Me and Haakon?" said BJ.

"Patrik," said Elea with a warning tone in her voice.

"Lise and I are over," he said, not looking too unhappy about it. "She's seeing some hotshot actor now. Met him on the set of The Torminator, apparently. Good for her."

Elea extended the back of the car so that they could all fit in, and they drove in silence to Dordi's house, dropping Petra, Sander and the little one off on the way.

Dordi and Torsten hugged wordlessly for a long time. Elea and Jan left them to it, promising to come back the next day. Dordi promised she would make dumplings.

"Is he …?" asked Torsten.

"He's dozing," said Dordi. "Just go in. He's expecting you."

Torsten tentatively opened the door to Arne's room. He was sleeping on the ground floor now so that Dordi didn't have to run up and down the stairs to take care of him. As he entered, he had an intense feeling of déjà vu. Arne was sitting in bed propped up on a mountain of pillows, looking for all the world like Zeus, minus the hair and beard. Arne was shocked to see how old and ill he looked. However, he cracked a smile the minute he opened his eyes and saw Torsten standing there.

"About dritting time," he said. "Did you bring me a present?"

"Actually, I did," said Torsten, producing a bottle of wine from the old, battered leather satchel he was wearing slung over his shoulder.

"Best you'll ever taste, I can guarantee it."

"Better open it then," grinned Arne. "We'll drink a toast to your safe return."

"And to old friends," smiled Torsten, glad to see his old friend in such good spirits despite his frail appearance.

"Don't suppose you have a corkscrew around here, do you?"

"Look in that sideboard over there," said Arne. "There should be one and a couple of glasses too."

Torsten thought it was weird that there should be a sideboard in Arne's bedroom, but then remembered that this used to be a dining room before Arne got ill, and Dordi turned it into a spare bedroom.

"Are you sure about this?" said Torsten, opening the bottle. "Dordi may well kill us."

"Well, I'm dying anyway," wheezed Arne, "so I get a free pass."

Torsten didn't know whether to laugh or cry. He poured two glasses of wine and handed one to Arne, who sniffed it appreciatively and then took a good gulp, which set off a coughing fit that scared Torsten half to death.

"Should I fetch Dordi?" he asked in a blind panic, heading for the door as his friend gasped for breath.

"No, no … I'll be fine," Arne managed to choke out. "Come and sit down next to me."

Torsten sat in the chair by the bed. Once Arne had recovered sufficiently, he said, "That is a dritting good glass of wine."

"Dionysus's best," said Torsten. "He's the God of wine. And theatre."

Arne looked at him blankly.

Torsten downed the rest of his wine in one gulp and said, "Arne, my friend, open your ear holes because I have got so much to tell you."

CHAPTER FIFTEEN

The final chapter

"Wow," said Petra, turning over the final page of Torsten's book.

"Wow good or wow bad?" said Torsten, barely daring to breathe.

"Wow *very* good," said Petra, pink-faced with pleasure.

Torsten breathed. After Arne's death, he had returned to his hermit-like existence in Bestefar's cottage and had thrown himself heart and soul into rewriting his lost manuscript. BJ had told Petra all about Homer and the fact that Haakon had nicked off with Bestefar's notebook. She had expressed an interest in reading the story should Torsten ever have the courage and the memory to reproduce it, and now here they were.

"I don't like the title so much though," said Petra. "I mean, "The Olympic Games"?"

"It has a double meaning," said Torsten. "The games that the Gods play, and the games that the Gods play ... oh ... I know what I mean."

"That might be a little deep," said Petra. "How about we just call it "Olympus"? It's a bit snappier for a Netteflix series. I think it'll have more popular appeal."

"You know best," said Torsten.

"I do really like the dedication, though," said Petra, opening the beginning of the book once again and reading, "To those we have loved and lost."

"I'm going to make a game out of it," said BJ. "But I still prefer "Limp Puss", as names go."

"Seriously, BJ?" squeaked Petra and Torsten simultaneously.

BJ shrugged and said, "Freki would've liked it."

"Ah likes it," said Xenia, sashaying into Petra's office with a tray full of cups of coffee.

"Thanks, babe," said BJ, and blew her a kiss.

<u>*An Epic Epilogue*</u>

750 BC, Ancient Greece. A young goatherd by the name of Leon seeks shelter from a storm in a small cave near the foot of the north face of Mount Olympus. He takes a piece of bread from the pocket of his tunic and munches on it thoughtfully, waiting for the storm to pass. Suddenly, something at the back of the cave catches his eye.

Leon has never seen parchment before. He is fascinated by the texture of it and by the peculiar squiggles, loops and curls covering almost the entire surface. He traces them with one dirty finger. Somehow, deep in his being, he knows that he has stumbled upon something very important.

There is something else lying amidst the debris at the back of the cave. It is thicker than the parchment and looks more substantial. However, as Leon tries to pick it up, he just has time to see some vague symbols seemingly scratched onto the surface before it crumbles to dust in his hands.

As soon as the storm abates, Leon leaves his goats and hurries to take the pile of parchments to his father, a slave, who promptly passes it on to his master. It finally reaches the upper echelons of ancient Greek society and sparks off a religious frenzy and a sudden, superstitious surge of belief in the Olympian Gods and their supernatural powers, leading to the building of temples, countless numbers of sacrifices and endless speculation on just who this Homer person was anyway.

Much, much later, the contents of the parchments are printed in millions of copies and a multitude of languages. Sadly, due to scorch marks or dirt obscuring certain parts of the text, they are misread and Lidia becomes "Iliad", and "Odd Sea", the "Odyssey".

And the rest, as they say, is mythology.

THE END

About the Author

Josephine Draycott was born in Singapore to English parents and lived in the UK until she completed her university studies in modern languages and went on an exchange visit to Belgium, where she has lived ever since.

This is Josephine's third foray into the world of book writing after "Who knew the storm" and "Who knew the storm: The New Generation." It is the third and final part of the trilogy, and she has immensely enjoyed writing it.

She is now a primary school teacher and sincerely believes that there is at least one book inside of everyone.

9 781916 849877